Boy Scouts in the Rockies

by

Edwin L. Sabin

CHAPTER I

THE LONG TRAIL

We are the Elk Patrol, 14th Colorado Troop, Boy Scouts of America. Our sign is and our colors are dark green and white, like the pines and the snowy range. Our patrol call is the whistle of an elk, which is an "Ooooooooooooo!" high up in the head, like a locomotive whistle. We took the Elk brand (that is the same as totem, you know, only we say "brand," in the West), because elks are the great trail-makers in the mountains.

About the hardest thing that we have set out to do yet has been to carry a secret message across the mountains, one hundred miles, from our town to another town, with our own pack outfit, and finding our own trail, and do it in fifteen days including Sundays. That is what I want to tell about, in this book.

There were six of us who went; and just for fun we called ourselves by trapper or scout names. We were:

First-class Scout Roger Franklin, or General William Ashley. He is our patrol leader. He is fifteen years old, and red-headed, and his mother is a widow and keeps a boarding-house.

First-class Scout Tom Scott, or Major Andrew Henry. He is our corporal. He is sixteen years old, and has snapping black eyes, and his father is mayor.

First-class Scout Harry Leonard, or Kit Carson. He is thirteen years old, and before he came into the Scouts we called him "Sliver" because he's so skinny. His father is a groceryman.

First-class Scout Chris Anderson, or Thomas Fitzpatrick the Bad Hand. He is fifteen years old, and tow-headed and all freckled, and has only half a left arm. He got hurt working in the mine. But he's as smart as any of us.

He can use a camera and throw a rope and dress himself, and tie his shoe-laces and other knots. He's our best trailer. His father is a miner.

Second-class Scout Richard Smith, or Jedediah Smith. He is only twelve, and is a "fatty," and his father is postmaster.

Second-class Scout Charley Brown, or Jim Bridger the Blanket Chief. That's myself. I'm fourteen, and have brown eyes and big ears, and myfather is a lawyer. When we started I had just been promoted from a tenderfoot, so I didn't know very much yet. But we're all first-class Scouts now, and have honors besides.

For Scout work we were paired off like this: Ashley and Carson; Henry and Smith; Fitzpatrick and Bridger.

Our trip would have been easier (but it was all right, anyway), if a notice hadn't got into the newspaper and put other boys up to trying to stop us. This is what the notice said:

The Elk Patrol of the local Boy Scouts is about to take a message from Mayor Scott across the range to the mayor of Green Valley. This message will be sealed and in cipher, and the boys will be granted fifteen days in which to perform the trip over, about 100 miles, afoot; so they will have to hustle. They must not make use of any vehicles or animals except their pack-animals, or stop at ranches except through injury or illness, but must pursue their own trail and live off the country. The boys who will go are Roger Franklin, Tom Scott, Dick Smith, Harry Leonard, Chris Anderson, and Charley Brown.

Of course, this notice gave the whole scheme away, and some of the other town boys who pretended to make fun of us Scouts because we were trying to learn Scoutcraft and to use it right planned to cut us off and take the message away from us. There always are boys mean enough to bother and interfere, until they get to be Scouts themselves. Then they are ashamed.

We knew that we were liable to be interfered with, because we heard some talk, and Bill Duane (he's one of the town fellows; he doesn't do much of anything except loaf) said to me: "Oh, you'll never get through, kid. The bears will eat you up. Bears are awful bad in that country."

But this didn't scare us. Bears aren't much, if you let them alone. We knew what he meant, though. And we got an anonymous letter. It came to General Ashley, and showed a skull and cross-bones, and said:

BEWARE!!! No Boy Scouts allowed on the Medicine Range! Keep Off!!!

That didn't scare us, either.

When we were ready to start, Mayor Scott called us into his office and told us that this was to be a real test of how we could be of service in time of need and of how we could take care of ourselves; and that we were carrying a message to Garcia, and must get it through, if we could, but that he put us on our honor as Scouts to do just as we had agreed to do.

Then we saluted him, and he saluted us with a military salute, and we gave our Scouts' yell, and went.

Our Scouts' yell is:

B. S. A.! B. S. A.!

Elk! Elk! Hoo-ray!!

and a screech all together, like the bugling of an elk.

This is how we marched. The message was done up flat, between cardboard covered by oiled silk with the Elk totem on it, and was slung by a buckskin thong from the general's neck, under his shirt, out of sight.

We didn't wear coats, because coats were too hot, and you can't climb with your arms held by coat-sleeves. We had our coats in the packs, for emergencies. We wore blue flannel shirts with the Scouts' emblem on the sleeves, and Scouts' drab service hats, and khaki trousers tucked into mountain-boots hob-nailed with our private pattern so that we could tell each other's tracks, and about our necks were red bandanna handkerchiefs knotted loose, and on our hands were gauntlet gloves. Little Jed Smith, who is a fatty, wore two pairs of socks, to prevent his feet from blistering. That is a good scheme.

General Ashley and Major Henry led; next were our two burros, Sally (who was a yellow burro with a white spot on her back) and Apache (who was a black burro and was named for Kit Carson's—the real Kit Carson's—favorite horse). Behind the burros we came: the two other first-class Scouts, and then the second-class Scouts, who were Jed Smith and myself.

We took along two flags: one was the Stars and Stripes and the other was our Patrol flag—green with a white Elk totem on it. They were fastened to a jointed staff, the Stars and Stripes on top and the Patrol flag below; and the butt of the staff was sharpened, to stick into the ground. The flags flew in camp. We did not have tents. We had three tarps, which are tarpaulins or cowboy canvas bed-sheets, to sleep in, on the ground, and some blankets and quilts for over and under, too. And these and our cooking things and a change of underclothes and stockings, etc., were packed on the burros with panniers and top-packs lashed tight with the diamond hitch.

We decided to pack along one twenty-two caliber rifle, for rabbits when we needed meat. One gun is enough in a camp of kids. This gun was under the general's orders (he was our leader, you know), so that there wouldn't be any promiscuous shooting around in the timber, and somebody getting hit. It was for business, not monkey-work. We took one of our bows, the short and thick Indian kind, and some of our two-feathered arrows, in case that we must get meat without making any noise. And we had two lariat ropes. Each pair of Scouts was allotted a war-bag, to hold their personal duds, and each fellow put in a little canvas kit containing tooth-brush and powder, comb and brush, needles and thread, etc.

For provisions we had flour, salt, sugar, bacon, dried apples, dried potatoes, rice, coffee (a little), tea, chocolate, baking-powder, condensed milk, canned butter, and half a dozen cans of beans, for short order. Canned stuff is heavy, though, and mean to pack. We didn't fool with raw beans, in bulk. They use much space, and at 10,000 and 12,000 feet they take too long to soak and cook.

We depended on catching trout, and on getting rabbits or squirrels to tide us over; and we were allowed to stock up at ranches, if we should pass any. That was legitimate. Even the old trappers traded for meat from the Indians.

We had our first-aid outfits—one for each pair of us. I carried Chris's and mine. We were supplied with camp remedies, too. Doctor Wallace of our town, who was our Patrol surgeon, had picked them out for us.

General Ashley and Major Henry set the pace. The trail out of town was good, and walking fast and straight-footed we trailed by the old stage road four miles, until we came to Grizzly Gulch. Here we turned off, by a prospectors' trail, up Grizzly. The old stage road didn't go to Green Valley. Away off to the northwest, now, was the Medicine Range that we must cross, to get at Green Valley on the other side. It is a high, rough range, 13,000 and 14,000 feet, and has snow on it all the year. In the middle was Pilot Peak, where we expected to strike a pass.

The prospect trail was fair, and we hustled. We didn't stop to eat much, at noon; that would have taken our wind. The going was up grade and you can't climb fast on a full stomach. We had a long march ahead of us, for old Pilot Peak looked far and blue.

Now and then the general let us stop, to puff for a moment; and the packs had to be tightened after Sally's and Apache's stomachs had gone down with exercise. We followed the trail single file, and about two o'clock, by the sun, we reached the head of the gulch and came out on top of the mesa there.

We were hot and kind of tired (especially little Jed Smith, our "fatty"); but we were not softies and this was no place to halt long. We must cross and get under cover again. If anybody was spying on us we could be seen too easy, up here. When you're pursuing, you keep to the high ground, so as to see; but when you're pursued you keep to the low ground, so as not to be seen. That was the trappers' way.

I'll tell you what we did. There are two ways to throw pursuers off the scent. We might have done as the Indians used to do. They would separate, after a raid, and would spread out in a big fan-shape, every one making a trail of his own, so that the soldiers would not know which to follow; and after a long while they would come together again at some point which they had agreed on. But we weren't ready to do this. It took time, and we did not have any meeting-spot, exactly. So we left as big a trail as we could, to make any town gang think that we were not suspicious. That would throw them off their guard.

Single file we traveled across the mesa, and at the other side we dipped into a little draw. Here we found Ute Creek, which we had planned to follow up to its headwaters in the Medicine Range. A creek makes a good guide. A cow-trail ran beside it.

"First-class Scout Fitzpatrick (that was Chris) and Second-class Scout Bridger (that was I) drop out and watch the trail," commanded General Ashley (that was Patrol Leader Roger Franklin). "Report at Bob Cat Springs. We'll camp there for the night."

Chris and I knew what to do. We gave a big leap aside, to a flat rock, and the other Scouts continued right along; and because they were single file the trail didn't show any difference. I don't suppose that the town gang would have noticed, anyway; but you must never despise the enemy.

From the flat rock Fitzpatrick and I stepped lightly, so as not to leave much mark, on some dried grass, and made off up the side of the draw, among the bushes. These grew as high as our shoulders, and formed a fine ambuscade. We climbed far enough so that we could see both sides of the draw and the trail in between; and by crawling we picked a good spot and sat down.

We knew that we must keep still, and not talk. We kept so still that field-mice played over our feet, and a bee lit on Fitzpatrick. He didn't brush it off.

We could talk sign language; that makes no sound. Of course, Fitz could talk with only one hand. He made the signs to watch down the trail, and to listen; and I replied with men on horseback and be vigilant as a wolf.

It wasn't bad, sitting here in the sunshine, amidst the brush. The draw was very peaceful and smelled of sage. A magpie flew over, his black and white tail sticking out behind him; and he saw us and yelled. Magpies are awful sharp, that way. They're a good sign to watch. Everything tells something to a Scout, when he's an expert.

Sitting there, warm and comfortable, a fellow felt like going to sleep; but Fitzpatrick was all eyes and ears, and I tried to be the same, as a Scout should.

CHAPTER II

THE NIGHT ATTACK

We must have been squatting for an hour and a half, and the sun was down close to the top of the draw, behind us, when Fitzpatrick nudged me with his foot, and nodded. He made the sign of birds flying up and pointed down the trail, below, us; so that I knew somebody was coming, around a turn there.   We scarcely breathed. We just sat and watched, like two mountain lions waiting.

Pretty soon they came riding along—four of them on horseback; we knew the horses. The fellows were Bill Duane, Mike Delavan, Tony Matthews, and Bert Hawley. They were laughing and talking because the trail we made was plain and they thought that we all were pushing right on, and if they could read sign they would know that the tracks were not extra fresh.

We let them get out of sight; then we went straight down upon the trail, and followed, alongside, so as not to step on top of their tracks and show that we had come after.

We talked only by sign, and trailed slow, because they might be listening or looking back. We wanted to find where they stopped. At every turn we sneaked and Fitzpatrick stuck just his head around, to see that the trail was clear. Suddenly he made sign to me that he saw them; there were three on horseback, waiting, and one had gone on, walking, to reconnoiter.

So we had to back-trail until we could make a big circle and strike the trail on ahead. This wasn't open country here; there were cedars and pinyons and big rocks. We circuited up and around, out of sight from the trail, and came in, bending low and walking carefully so as not to crack sticks, to listen and examine for sign. We found strange tracks—soles without hob-nails, pointing one way but not coming back. We hid behind a cedar, and waited. In about fifteen minutes Bill Duane walked right past us, back to the other fellows.

Now we hurried on, for it was getting dark; and soon we smelled smoke, and that meant camp. Fitzpatrick (who was a first-class Scout, while I was only a second) reported to General Ashley the whereabouts of the enemy.

"Very well," said General Ashley. "Corporal Andrew Henry (that was Tom Scott) and Second-class Scout Jed Smith (that was Dick Smith) will go back a quarter of a mile and picket the trail until relieved; the rest of us will proceed with camp duties."

Major Henry and little Jed Smith set off. We finished establishing camp. Two holes were dug for camp refuse; that was my business. Places for the beds were cleared of sticks and things; that was Kit Carson's business. General Ashley chopped a cedar stump for wood (cedar burns without soot, you know); and Fitzpatrick cooked. The burros had been unpacked and the flags planted before Fitzpatrick and I came in. We had to picket the burros out, to graze, at first, or they might have gone back to town. Of course, as we were short-handed, we had to do Henry's and Smith's work, to-night, too: spread the beds before dark and bring water and such things.

For supper we had bacon and two cans of the beans and biscuits baked in a reflector, and coffee. Major Henry and Jed Smith were not getting any supper yet, because they were still on picket duty. But when we were through General Ashley said, "Kit Carson, you and Jim Bridger relieve Henry and Smith, and tell them to come in to supper."

But just as we stood, to start, Major Henry walked in amongst us. He was excited, and puffing, and he almost forgot to salute General Ashley, who was Patrol leader.

"They're planning to come!" he puffed. "I sneaked close to them and heard 'em talking!"

"Is this meant for a report?" asked General Ashley. And we others snickered. It wasn't the right way to make a report.

"Yes, sir," answered Henry. "That is, I reconnoitered the enemy's camp, sir, and they're talking about us."

"What did you hear?"

"They're going to rush us when we're asleep, and scare us."

"Very well," said General Ashley. "But you weren't ordered to do that. You left your post, sir."

"I thought you'd like to know. They didn't hear me," stammered Major Henry.

"You'd no business to go, just the same. Orders are orders. Where is Smith?"

"Watching on picket."

"Did he go, too?"

"No, sir."

"You exceeded orders, and you ought to be court-martialed," said General Ashley. And he was right, too. "But I'll give you another chance. When is the enemy going to attack?"

"After we're asleep."

"What is he doing now?"

"Eating and smoking and waiting, down the trail."

"You can have some coffee and beans and bread, while we hold council. Carson and Bridger can wait a minute."

The council didn't take long. General Ashley's plan was splendid, a joke and a counter-attack in one. Major Henry ate as much as he could, but he wasn't filled up when he was sent out again, into the dark, with Kit Carson. They were ordered to tell Jed Smith to come in, but they were to go on. You'll see what happened. This double duty was Henry's punishment.

We cleaned up the camp, and then Jed Smith arrived. While he was eating we made the beds. We drew up the tarpaulins, over blankets and quilts rolled so that the beds looked exactly as if we were in them, our feet to the fire (it was a little fire, of course) and our heads in shadow. We tied the burros short; and then we went back into the cedars and pinyons and sat down, quiet.

It wasn't pitchy dark. When the sky is clear it never gets pitchy dark, in the open; and there was a quarter-moon shining, too. The night was very still. The breeze just rustled the trees, but we could hear our hearts beat. Once, about a mile away, a coyote barked like a crazy puppy. He was calling for company. The stars twinkled down through the stiff branches, and I tried to see the Great Dipper, but that took too much squirming around.

We must not say a word, nor even whisper. We must just keep quiet, and listen and wait. Down the trail poor Major Henry and Kit Carson were having a harder time of it—but I would have liked to be along.

All of a sudden Fitzpatrick the Bad Hand nudged me gently with his knuckles, and I nudged Jed Smith, and Jed passed it on, and it went around from one to the other, so we all knew. Somebody was coming! We could hear a stick snap, and a little laugh, off in the timber; it sounded as though somebody had run into a branch. We waited. The enemy was stealing upon our camp. We hid our faces in our coats and our hands in our sleeves, so that no white should show. It was exciting, sitting this way, waiting for the attack.

The gang tiptoed up, carefully, and we could just make out two of them peering in at the beds. Then they all gave a tremendous yell, like Indians or mountain lions, and rushed us—or what they thought was us. They stepped on the beds and kicked at the tinware, and expected to scare us stiff with the noise—but you ought to have seen how quick they quit when nothing happened! We didn't pop out of the beds, and run! It was funny— and I almost burst, trying not to laugh out loud, when they stood, looking about, and feeling of the beds again.

"They aren't here," said Bill Duane. At a nudge from General Ashley we had deployed, running low and swift, right and left.

"Poke the fire, so we can see," said Bert Hawley.

One of them did, so the fire blazed up—which was just what we wanted. Now they were inside and we were outside. They began to talk.

"We'll pile up the camp, anyway."

"They're around somewhere."

"Let's take their burros."

"Take their flags."

Then General Ashley spoke up.

"No, you don't!" he said. "You let those things alone."

That voice, coming out of the darkness around, must have made them jump, and for a minute they didn't know what to do. Then—

"Why?" asked Bill Duane, kind of defiantly.

"Wait a moment and we'll show you," answered General Ashley.

He whistled loud, our Scouts' signal whistle; and off down the trail Major Henry or Kit Carson whistled back, and added the whistle that meant "All right."

"Hear that?" asked General Ashley. "That means we've got your horses!"

Hurrah! So we had. You see, Major Henry and Kit Carson had been sent back to watch the enemy's camp; and when the gang had left, on foot, to surprise us, our two scouts had gone in and captured the horses. We couldn't help but whoop and yell a little, in triumph. But General Ashley ordered "Silence!" and we quit.

"Aw, we were just fooling," said Tony Matthews. They talked together, low, for a few moments; and Bill called: "Come on in. We won't hurt you."

"Of course you won't," said General Ashley. "But we aren't fooling. We mean business. We'll keep the horses until you've promised to clear out and let this camp alone."

"We don't want the horses. Two of 'em are hired and the longer you keep them the more you'll have to pay." That was a lie. They didn't hire horses. They borrowed.

"We can sleep here very comfortably, kid," said Mike Delavan.

"You'll not get much sleep in those beds," retorted General Ashley. "Will they, boys!"

And we all laughed and said "No!"

"And after they've walked ten miles back to town, we'll bring in the horses and tell how we took them."

The enemy talked together low, again.

"All right," said Bill Duane. "You give us our horses and we'll let the camp alone."

"Do you promise?" asked General Ashley.

"Yes; didn't I say so?"

"Do you, Mike?"

"Sure; if you return those horses."

"Do you, Tony and Bert?"

"Uh huh."

That was the best way—to make each promise separately; for some one of them might have claimed that he hadn't promised with the rest.

"Then go on down the trail, and you'll find the horses where you left them."

"How do we know?"

"On the honor of a Scout," said General Ashley. "We won't try any tricks, and don't you, for we'll be watching you until you start for town."

They grumbled back, and with Bill Duane in the lead stumbled for the trail. General Ashley whistled the signal agreed upon, for Major Henry and Kit Carson to tie the horses and to withdraw. We might have followed the enemy; but we would have risked dividing our forces too much and leaving the camp. We were safer here.

So we waited, quiet; and after a time somebody signaled with the whistle of the patrol. It was Kit Carson.

"They've gone, sir," he reported, when General Ashley called him.

"What did they say?"

"They're mad; but they're going into town and they'll get back at us later."

"You saw them start, did you?"

"Yes, sir."

"Where's Henry?"

"Waiting to see if they turn or anything."

"They won't. They know we'll be ready for them. Shall we move camp, or post sentries, boys?"

We voted to post sentries. It seemed an awful job to move camp, at this time of night, and make beds over again, and all that. It was only ten o'clock by General Ashley's watch, but it felt later. So we built up the fire, and set some coffee on, and called Major Henry in, and General Ashley and Jed Smith took the first spell of two hours; then they were to wake up Fitzpatrick and me, for the next two hours; and Major Henry and Kit Carson would watch from two till four, when it would be growing light. But we didn't have any more trouble that night.

CHAPTER III

THE BIG TROUT

It was mighty hard work, turning out at five o'clock in the morning. That was regulations, while on the march—to get up at five. The ones who didn't turn out promptly had to do the dirty work—police the camp, which is to clean it, you know.

Fitzpatrick the Bad Hand cooked; I helped, by opening packages, preparing potatoes (if we had them), tending fire, etc.; Major Henry chopped wood; Kit Carson and little Jed Smith looked after the burros, Apache and Sally, and scouted in a circle for hostile sign; General Ashley put the bedding in shape to pack.

But first it was regulations to take a cold wet rub when we were near water. It made us glow and kept us in good shape. Then we brushed our teeth and combed our hair. After breakfast we policed the camp, and dumped everything into a hole, or burned it, so that we left the place just about as we had found it. We stamped out the fire, or put dirt and water on it, of course. Then we packed the burros. General Ashley, Jed Smith, and Kit Carson packed Sally; Major Henry, Thomas Fitzpatrick, and I packed Apache. And by six-thirty we were on our way.

This morning we kept on up Ute Creek. It had its rise in Gray Bull Basin, at the foot of old Pilot Peak, about forty miles away. We thought we could make Gray Bull Basin in three days. Ten or twelve miles a day, with burros, on the trail, up-hill all the way, is about as fast as Scouts like us can keep going. Beyond Gray Bull we would have to find our own trail over Pilot Peak.

Everything was fine, this morning. Birds were hopping among the cedars and spruces, and in some places the ground was red with wild strawberries. Pine squirrels scolded at us, and we saw two rabbits; but we didn't stop to shoot them. We had bacon, and could catch trout higher up the creek. Here were some beaver dams, and around the first dam lived a big trout that nobody had been able to land. The beaver dams were famous camping places for parties who could go this far, and everybody claimed to have hooked the big trout and to have lost him again. He was a native Rocky Mountain trout, and weighed four pounds—but he was educated. He wouldn't be caught. He had only one eye; that was how people knew him.

We didn't count upon that big trout, but we rather counted upon some smaller ones; and anyway we must hustle on and put those ten miles behind us before the enemy got in touch with us again. Our business was to carry that message through, and not to stop and hunt or lose time over uncalled-for things.

The creek foamed and rushed; its water was amber, as if stained by pine needles. Sometimes it ran among big bowlders, and sometimes it was crossed by fallen trees. Thomas Fitzpatrick picked up a beaver cutting. That was an aspen stick (beavers like aspen and willow bark best) about as large as your wrist and two feet long. It was green and the ends were fresh, so there were beavers above us. And it wasn't water-soaked, so that it could not have been cut and in the water very long. We were getting close.

We traveled right along, and the country grew rougher. There were many high bowlders, and we came to a canyon where the creek had cut between great walls like a crack. There was no use in trying to go through this canyon; the trail had faded out, and we were about to oblique off up the hill on our side of the creek, to go around and strike the creek above the canyon, when Kit Carson saw something caught on a brush-heap half in the water, at the mouth of the canyon.

It was a chain. He leaned out and took hold of the chain, and drew it in to shore. On the other end was a trap, and in the trap was a beaver. The chain was not tied to the brush; it had just caught there, so it must have been washed down. Then up above somebody was trapping beaver, which was against the law. The beaver was in pretty bad condition. He must have been drowned for a week or more. The trap had no brand on it. Usually traps are branded on the pan, but this wasn't and that went to show that whoever was trapping knew better. The sight of that beaver, killed uselessly, made us sick and mad both. But we couldn't do anything about it, except to dig a hole and bury trap and all, so that the creek would wash clean, as it ought to be. Then we climbed up the steep hill, over rocks and flowers, and on top followed a ridge, until ahead we saw the creek again. It was in a little meadow here, and down we went for it.

This was a beautiful spot. On one side the pines and spruces covered a long slope which rose on and on until above timber line it was bare and reddish gray; and away up were patches of snow; and beyond was the tip of Pilot Peak. But on our side a forest fire had burned out the timber, leaving only black stumps sticking up, with the ground covered by a new growth of bushes. There was quite a difference between the two sides; and we camped where we were, on the bare side, which was the safest for a camp fire. It would have been a shame to spoil the other side, too.

We were tired, after being up part of the night and climbing all the morning, and this was a good place to stop. Plenty of dry wood, plenty of water, and space to spread our beds.

The creek was smooth and wide, here, about the middle of the park. The beaver had been damming it. But although we looked about, after locating camp and unpacking the burros, we couldn't find a fresh sign. We came upon camp sign, though, two days old, at least. Somebody had trapped every beaver and then had left.

That seemed mean, because it was against the law to trap beaver, and here they weren't doing any harm. But the fire had laid waste one shore of the pond, and animal killers had laid waste the pond itself.

We decided to have a big meal. There ought to be wild raspberries in this burnt timber; wild raspberries always follow a forest fire—and that is a queer thing, isn't it? So, after camp was laid out (which is the first thing to do), and our flags set up, while Fitzpatrick the Bad Hand and Major Henry built a fire and got things ready for dinner, General Ashley and Kit Carson went after berries and little Jed Smith and I were detailed to catch trout.

We had lines and hooks, but we didn't bother to pack rods, because you almost always can get willows. Some fellows would have cut green willows, because they bend. We knew better. We cut a dead willow apiece. We were after meat, and not just sport; and when we had a trout bite we wanted to yank him right out. A stiff, dead willow will do that. Grasshoppers were whirring around, among the dried trunks and the grass. That is what grasshoppers like, a place where it's hot and open. As a rule you get bigger fish with bait than you do with a fly, so we put on grasshoppers. I hate sticking a hook into a grasshopper, or a worm either; and we killed our grasshoppers quick by smashing their heads before we hooked them.

It was going to be hard work, catching trout around this beaver pond. The water was wide and smooth and shallow and clear, and a trout would see you coming. When a trout knows that you are about, then the game is off. Besides, lots of people had been fishing the pond, and the beaver hunters must have been fishing it lately, according to sign. But that made it all the more exciting. Little trout are caught easily, and the big ones are left for the person who can outwit them.

After we were ready, we reconnoitered. We sat down and studied to see where we'd prefer to be if we were a big trout. A big trout usually doesn't prowl about much. He gets a lair, in a hole or under a bank, and stays close, eating whatever comes his way, and chasing out all the smaller trout. Sometimes he swims into the ripples, to feed; but back he goes to his lair again.

So we studied the situation. There was no use in wading about, or shaking the banks, and scaring trout, unless we had a plan. It looked to me that if I were a big trout I'd be in a shady spot over across, where the water swept around a low place of the dam and made a black eddy under the branches of a spruce. Jed Smith said all right, I could try that, and he would try where the bank on our side stuck out over the water a little.

I figured that my hole would be fished by about everybody from the water. Most persons would wade across, and cast up-stream to the edge of it; and if a trout was still there he would be watching out for that. So the way to surprise him would be to sneak on him from a new direction. I went down below, and crossed (over my boot-tops) to the other side, and followed up through the timber.

I had to crawl under the spruce—and I was mighty careful not to shake the ground or to make any noise, for we needed fish. Nobody had been to the hole from this direction; it was too hard work. By reaching out with my pole I could just flip the hopper into the water. I tried twice; and the second time I landed him right in the swirl. He hadn't floated an inch when a yellowish thing calmly rose under him and he was gone!

I jerked up with the willow, and the line tightened and began to tug. I knew by the color and the way he swallowed the hopper without any fuss that he was a king trout, and if I didn't haul him right in he'd break the pole or tear loose. I shortened pole like lightning and grabbed the line; but it got tangled in the branches of the spruce, and the trout was hung up with just his nose out of water.

Jiminy! but he was making the spray fly. He looked as big as a beaver, and the hook was caught in the very edge of his lip. That made me hurry. In a moment he'd be away. I suppose I leaned out too far, to grab the line again, or to get him by the gills, for I slipped and dived headfirst into the hole.

Whew, but the water was cold! It took my breath—but I didn't care. All I feared was that now I'd lost the fish. He weighed four pounds, by this time, I was sure. As soon as I could stand and open my eyes I looked for him. When I had dived in I must have shaken loose the line, for it was under water again, and part of the pole, too. I sprawled for the pole and grabbed it as it was sliding out. The line tightened. The trout was still on.

Now I must rustle for the shore. So I did, paying out the pole behind me so as not to tear the hook free; and the minute I scrambled knee-deep, with a big swing I hustled that trout in and landed him in the brush just as he flopped off!

I tell you, I was glad. Some persons would have wanted a reel and light tackle, to play him — but we were after meat.

"I've got one — a big one!" I yelled, across to where Jed Smith was.

"So have I!" yelled little Jed back.

I had picked my trout up. He wasn't so awful big, after all; only about fifteen inches long, which means two pounds. He was an Eastern brook trout. They grow larger in the cold water of the West than they do in their own homes. But I looked for Jed — and then dropped my trout and waded over to help him.

He was out in the water, up to his waist, and something was jerking him right along.

"I can't get him out!" he called, as I was coming. "How big is yours?"

"Fifteen inches."

"This one's as big as I am — big native!" And you should have heard Jed grunt, as the line just surged around, in the current.

"Want any help?" I asked.

"Uh uh. If he can lick me, then he ought to get away."

"Where'd you catch him?"

"Against the bank."

"Swing him down the current and then lift him right in shore!"

"Look out he doesn't tear loose!"

"He'll break that pole!"

Fitzpatrick and Major Henry were yelling at us from the fire; and then Jed stubbed his toe on a rock and fell flat. He didn't let the pole go, though. He came up sputtering and he was as wet as I.

"Swing him down and then lift him right in!" kept shouting Fitz and Major Henry. That was the best plan.

"All right," answered Jed. "You take the pole and start him," he said to me. "I'd have to haul him against the current." I was below him, of course, so as to head the trout up-stream.

He tossed the butt at me and I caught it. That was generous of Jed — to let me get the fish out, when he'd been the one to hook it. But we were Scouts together, and we were after meat for all, not glory for one.

I took the pole and with a swing downstream kept Mr. Trout going until he shot out to the edge of the pond, and there Fitz tumbled on top of him and grabbed him with one hand by the gills.

When we held him up we gave our Patrol yell:

B. S. A.! B. S. A.!

Elks! Elks! Hoo-ray!

Ooooooooooooo!

CHAPTER IV

THE BEAVER MAN

For he was a great one, that trout! He was the big fellow that everybody had been after, because he was twenty-six inches long and weighed four pounds and had only one eye! That was good woodcraft, for a boy twelve years old to sneak up on him and catch him with a willow pole and a line tied fast and a grasshopper, when regular fishermen with fine outfits had been trying right along. Of course they'll say we didn't give him any show—but after he was hooked there was no use in torturing him. The hooking is the principal part.

Jed showed us how he had worked. He hadn't raised anything in the first hole, by the bank, and he had gone on to another place that looked good. Lots of people had fished this second place; there was a regular path to it through the weeds, on the shore side; and below it, along the shallows, the mud was full of tracks. But Jed had been smart. A trout usually lies with his head up-stream, so as to gobble whatever comes down. But here the current set in with a back-action, so that it made a little eddy right against the bank—and a trout in that particular spot would have his nosedownstream. So Jed fished from the direction opposite to that from which other persons had fished. He went around, and approached from up-stream, awfully careful not to make any noise or raise any settlings. Then he reached far and bounced his hopper from the bank into the edge — as if it had fallen of itself—and it was gobbled quick as a wink and the old trout pulled Jed in, too.

So in fishing as in other scouting, I guess, you ought to do what the enemy isn't expecting you to do.

My trout was just a minnow beside of Jed's; and the two of them were all we could eat, so we quit; Jed and I stripped off our wet clothes and took a rub with a towel and sat in dry underclothes, while the wet stuff was hung up in the sun. We felt fine.

That was a great dinner. We rolled the trout in mud and baked them whole. And we had fried potatoes, hot bread (or what people would call biscuits), and wild raspberries with condensed milk. General Ashley and Kit Carson had brought in a bucket of them. They were thick, back in the burnt timber, and were just getting ripe.

After the big dinner and the washing of the dishes we lay around resting. Jed Smith and I couldn't do much until our clothes were dry. We stuffed our boots with some newspapers we had, to help them dry. While we were resting, Fitzpatrick made our "Sh!" sign which said "Watch out! Danger!" and with his hand by his side pointed across the beaver pond.

We looked, with our eyes but not moving, so as not to attract attention. Yes, a man had stepped out to the edge of the timber, at the upper end of the pond and across, and was standing. Maybe he thought we didn't see him, but we did. And he saw us, too; for after a moment he stepped back again, and was gone. He had on a black slouch hat. He wasn't a large man.

We pretended not to have noticed him, until we were certain that he wasn't spying from some other point. Then General Ashley spoke, in a low tone: "He acted suspicious. We ought to reconnoiter. Scouts Fitzpatrick and Bridger will circle around the upper end of the pond, and Scout Kit Carson and I will circle the lower. Scouts Corporal Henry and Jed Smith will guard camp."

My boots were still wet, but I didn't mind. So we started off, in pairs, which was the right way, Fitz and I for the upper end of the pond. I carried a pole, as if we were going fishing, and we didn't hurry. We sauntered through the brush, and where the creek was narrow we crossed on some rocks, and followed the opposite shore down, a few yards back, so as to cut the spy's tracks. I might not have found them, among the spruceneedles; but Fitzpatrick the Bad Hand did. He found a heel mark, and by stooping down and looking along we could see a line where the needles had been kicked up, to the shore. Marks show better, sometimes, when you look this way, along the ground; but we could have followed, anyhow, I think.

The footprints were plain in the soft sand; if he had stood back a little further, and had been more careful where he stepped, we might not have found the tracks so easily; but he had stepped on some soft sand and mud. We knew that he was not a large man, because we had seen him; and we didn't believe that he was a prospector or a miner, because his soles were not hobbed—or a cow-puncher, because he had no high heels to sink in; he may have been a rancher, out looking about.

"He must be left-handed," said Fitz.

"Why?" I asked.

"Because, see?" and then he told me.

Sure enough. That was smart of Fitz, I thought. But he's splendid to read sign.

Now we followed the tracks back. The man had come down and had returned by the same route. And up in the timber about fifty yards he had had a horse. We read how he had been riding through, and had stopped, and got off and walked down to the pond, and stood, and walked back and mounted again and ridden on. All that was easy for Fitz, and I could read most of it myself.

We trailed the horse until the tracks surely went away from the pond into the timber country; then we let it go, and met General Ashley, to report. General Ashley and Kit Carson also examined the prints in the sand, and we all agreed that the man probably was left-handed.

Now, why had he come down to the edge of the pond, on purpose, and looked at it and at us, and then turned up at a trot into the timber? It would seem as if he might have been afraid that we had seen him, and he didn't want to be seen. But all our guesses here and after we reached camp again didn't amount to much, of course.

We decided to stay for the night. It was a good camp place, and we wouldn't gain anything, maybe, by starting on, near night, and getting caught in the timber in the dark. And this would give the burros a good rest and a fill-up before their climb.

The burned stretch where we were was plumb full of live things—striped chipmunks, and pine squirrels, and woodpecker families. Fitzpatrick started in to take chipmunk pictures—and you ought to see how he can manage a camera with one hand. He holds it between his knees or else under his left arm, to draw the bellows out, and the rest is easy.

He scouted about and got some pictures of chipmunks real close, by waiting, and a picture of a woodpecker feeding young ones, at a hole in a dead pine stump. This was a good place for bear to come, after the berries; and we were hoping that one would amble in while we were there so that Fitz could take a picture of it, too. Bears don't hurt people unless people try to hurt them; and a bear would sooner have raspberries than have a man or boy, any day. Fitzpatrick thought that if he could get a good picture of a bear, out in the open, that would bring him a Scout's honor. Of course, chipmunk pictures help, too. But while we were resting and fooling and taking pictures, and General Ashley was bringing his diary and his map up to date, for record, we had another visitor.

A man came riding a dark bay horse, with white nose and white right fore foot, along our side of the beaver pond, and halted at our camp. The horse had left ear swallow-tailed and was branded with a Diamond Five on the right shoulder. The man wasn't the man we had seen across the pond, for he wore a sombrero, and was taller and had on overalls, and cow-puncher boots.

"Howdy?" he said.

"How are you?" we answered.

He sort of lazily dismounted, and yawned—but his sharp eyes were taking us and our camp all in.

"Out fishing?" he asked.

"No, sir. Passing through," said General Ashley.

"Going far?"

"Over to Green Valley."

"Walking?"

"Yes, sir."

"Good place for beaver, isn't it?"

"A bad place."

"That so? Used to be some about here. Couldn't catch any, eh?"

"We aren't trying. But it seems a bad place for beaver because the only one we have seen is a dead one in a trap."

The man waked up. "Whose trap?"

"We don't know." And the general went on to explain.

The man nodded. "I'm a deputy game warden," he said at last. "Somebody's been trapping beaver in here, and it's got to stop. Haven't seen any one pass through?"

We had. The general reported.

"Smallish man?"

"Yes, sir."

"Roan hoss branded quarter circle D on the left hip? Brass-bound stirrups?"

"We didn't see the horse; but we think the man was left-handed," said the general.

"Why?"

"He was left-footed, because there was a hole in the sole of the left shoe, and that would look as though he used his left foot more than his right. So we think he may be left-handed, too."

The game warden grunted. He eyed our flag.

"You kids must be regular Boy Scouts."

"We are."

"Then I reckon you aren't catching any beaver. All right, I'll look for a left-footed man, maybe left-handed. But it's this fellow on the roan hoss I'm after. He's been trying to sell pelts. There's no use my trailing him, to-day. But I'll send word ahead, and if you lads run across him let somebody know. Where are you bound for?"

The general told him.

"By way of Pilot Peak?"

"Yes, sir."

"Well, I'll tell you a short cut. You see that strip of young timber running up over the ridge? That's an old survey trail. It crosses to the other side. Over beyond you'll strike Dixon's Park and a ruined saw-mill. After that you can follow up Dixon's Creek."

We thanked him and he mounted and rode away.

CHAPTER V

TWO RECRUITS

When we got up in the morning, the mountains still had their night-caps on. White mist was floating low about their tips, and lying in the gulches like streams and lakes. Above timber-line, opposite us, was a long layer of cloud, with the top of old Pilot Peak sticking through.

This was a weather sign, although the sun rose clear and the sky was blue. Nightcaps are apt to mean a showery day. We took our wet rub, ate breakfast, policed the camp and killed the fire, and General Ashley put camphor and cotton against little Jed Smith's back tooth, to stop some aching. Maybe there was a hole in the tooth, or maybe Jed had just caught cold in it, after being wet; but he ought to have had his teeth looked into before he started out on the scout. Anyway, the camphor stopped the ache—and made him dance, too.

We crossed the creek, above the beaver pond, and struck off into the old survey trail that cut over the ridge. The brush was thick, and the trees had sprung up again, so that really it wasn't a regular trail unless you had known about it. The blazes on the side trees had closed over. But all the same, by watching the scars, and by keeping in the line where the trees always opened out, and by watching the sky as it showed before, we followed right along.

After we had been traveling about two hours, we heard thunder and that made us hustle the more, to get out of the thin timber, so that we would not be struck by lightning. The wind moaned through the trees. The rain was coming, sure.

The trail was diagonally up-hill, all the way, and if we had been cigarette smokers we wouldn't have had breath enough to hit the fast pace that General Ashley set. The burros had to trot, and it made little Jed Smith, who is kind of fat, wheeze; but we stuck it out and came to a flat place of short dried grass and bushes, with no trees. Here we stopped. We were about nine thousand feet up.

From where we were we could see the storm. It was flowing down along a bald-top mountain back from our camp at the beaver pond, and looked like gray smoke. The sun was just being swallowed. Well, all we could do was to wait and take it, and see how bad it was. We tied Sally and Apache to some bushes, but we didn't unpack them, of course. The tarps on top would keep the grub from getting wet.

The storm made a grand sight, as it rolled toward us, over the timber. And soon it was raining below us, down at the beaver pond—and then, with a drizzle and a spatter, the rain reached us, too.

We sat hunched, under our hats, and took it. We might have got under blankets—but that would have given us soaked blankets for night, unless we had stretched the tarps, too; and if we had stretched the tarps then the rest of our packs would have suffered. The best way is to crawl under a spruce, where the limbs have grown close to the ground. But not in a thunder storm. And it is better to be wet yourself and have a dry camp for night, than to be dry yourself and have a wet camp for night.

Anyway, the rain didn't hurt us. While it thundered and lightened and the drops pelted us well, we sang our Patrol song—which is a song like one used by the Black feet Indians:

"The Elk is our Medicine,

He makes us very strong.

The Elk is our Medicine,

The Elk is our Medicine,

The Elk is our Medicine,

He makes us very strong.

Ooooooooooooooooooooooooo!"

And when the thunder boomed we sang at it:

"The Thunder is our Medicine—"

to show that we weren't afraid of it.

The squall passed on over us, and when it had about quit we untied the burros and started on again. In just a minute we were warm and sweating and could shed our coats; and the sun came out hot to dry us off.

We crossed the ridge, and on the other side we saw Dixon's Park. We knew it was Dixon's Park, because the timber had been cut from it, and Dixon's Park had had a saw-mill twenty years ago.

Once this park had been grown over with trees, like the side of the ridge where we had been climbing; but that saw-mill had felled everything in sight, so that now there were only old stumps and dead logs. It looked like a graveyard. If the mill had been watched, as most mills are to-day, and had been made to leave part of the trees, then the timber would have grown again.

Down through the graveyard we went, and stopped for nooning at the little creek which ran through the bottom. There weren't any fish in this creek; the mill had killed the timber, and it had driven out the fish with sawdust. It was just a dead place, and there didn't seem to be even chipmunks.

We had nooning at the ruins of the mill. Tin cans and old boot soles and rusted pipe were still scattered about. We were a little tired, and more rain was coming, so we made a fire by finding dry wood underneath slabs and things, and had tea and bread and butter. That rested us. Little Jed Smith was only twelve years old, and we had to travel to suit him and not just to suit us bigger boys. I'm fourteen and Major Henry is sixteen. All the afternoon was showery; first we were dry, then we were wet; and there wasn't much fun about sloshing and slipping along; but we pegged away, and climbed out of Dixon's Park to the ridge beyond it. Now we could see old Pilot Peak plain, and keeping to the high ground we made for it. It didn't look to be very far away; but we didn't know, now, all the things that lay between.

The top of this ridge was flat, and the forest reserve people had been through and piled up the brush, so that a fire would not spread easily. That made traveling good, and we hiked our best. Down in a gulch beside us there was a stream: Dixon's Creek. But we kept to the high ground, with our eyes open for a good camping spot, for the dark would close in early if the rain did not quit. And nobody can pick a good camping place in the dark.

Regular rest means a great deal when you are traveling across country. Even cowboys will tell you that. They bed down as comfortably as they can, every time, on the round-up.

After a while we came to a circular little spot, hard and flat, where the timber had opened out. And General Ashley stopped and with a whirl dug in his heel as sign that we would camp here. There was wood and drainage and grass for the burros, and no danger of setting fire to the trees if we made a big fire. We had to carry water up from the creek below, but that was nothing.

Now we must hustle and get the camp in shape quick, before the things get wet. While Fitzpatrick picked out a spot for his fire and Major Henry chopped wood, two of us unpacked each burro. We put the things under a tarp, and I started to bring up the water, but General Ashley spoke.

"We're out of meat," he said. "You take the rifle and shoot a couple of rabbits. There ought to be rabbits about after the rain."

This suited me. He handed me the twenty-two rifle and five cartridges; out of those five cartridges I knew I could get two rabbits or else I wasn't any good as a hunter. The sun was shining once more, and the shadows were long in the timber, so I turned to hunt against the sun, and put my shadow behind me. Of course, that wouldn't make very much difference, because rabbits usually see you before you see them; but I was out after meat and must not miss any chances. There always is a right way and a wrong way.

This was a splendid time to hunt for rabbits, right after a rain. They come out then before dark, and nibble about. And you can walk on the wetness without much noise. Early morning and the evening are the best rabbit hours, anyway.

I walked quick and straight-footed, looking far ahead, and right and left, through the timber, to sight whatever moved. Yet I might be passing close to a rabbit, without seeing him, for he would be squatting. So I looked behind, too. And after I had walked about twenty minutes, I did see a rabbit. He was hopping, at one side, through the bushes; he gave only about three hops, and squatted, to let me pass. So I stopped stock-still, and drew up my rifle. He was about thirty yards away, and was just a bunch like a stone; but I held my breath and aimed at where his ears joined his head, and fired quick. He just kicked a little. That was a pretty good shot and I was glad, for I didn't want to hurt him and we had to have meat.

I hunted quite a while before I saw another rabbit. The next one was a big old buck rabbit, because his hind quarters around his tail were brown; young rabbits are white there. He hopped off, without stopping, and I whistled at him—wheet! Then he stopped, and I missed him. I shot over him, because I was in a hurry. I went across and saw where the bullet had hit. And he had ducked.

He hopped out of sight, through the brush; so I must figure where he probably would go. On beyond was a hilly place, with rocks, and probably he lived here—and rabbits usually make up-hill when they're frightened. So I took a circle, to cut him off; and soon he hopped again and squatted. This time I shot him through the head, where I aimed; so I didn't hurt him, either. I picked him up and was starting back for camp, because two rabbits were enough, when I heard somebody shouting. It didn't sound like a Scout's shout, but I answered and waited and kept answering, and in a few minutes a strange boy came running and walking fast through the trees. He carried a single-barrel shotgun.

He never would have seen me if I hadn't spoken; but when he wasn't more than ten feet from me I said: "What's the matter?"

He jumped and saw me standing. "Hello," he panted. "Was it you who was shooting and calling?"

"Yes."

"Why didn't you come on, then?" he scolded. He was angry.

"Because you were coming," I said. "I stood still and called back, to guide you."

"What did you shoot at?"

"Rabbits."

He hadn't seen them before, but now he saw them on the ground. "Aw, jiminy!" he exclaimed. "We've got something better than that, but we can't make a fire and our matches are all wet and so are our blankets, and we don't know what to do. There's another fellow with me. We're lost."

He was a sight; wet and dirty and sweaty from running, and scared.

"What are you doing? Camping?" I asked.

He nodded. "We started for Duck Lake, with nothing but blankets and what grub we could carry; but we got to chasing around and we missed the trail and now we don't know where we are. Gee, but we're wet and cold. Where's your camp?"

"Back on the ridge."

"Got a fire?"

"Uh huh," I nodded. "Sure."

"Come on," he said. "We'll go and get the other fellow and then we'll camp near you so as to have some fire."

"All right," I said.

He led off, and I picked up the rabbits and followed. He kept hooting, and the other boy answered, and we went down into the gulch where the creek flowed. Now, that was the dickens of a place to camp! Anybody ought to know better than to camp down at the bottom of a narrow gulch, where it is damp and nasty and dark. They did it because it was beside the water, and because there was some soft grass that they could lie on.

The other boy was about seventeen, and was huddled in a blanket, trying to scratch a match and light wet paper. He wore a big Colt's six-shooter on a cartridge belt about his waist.

"Come out, Bat," called the boy with me. "Here's a kid from another camp, where they have fire and things."

Bat grunted, and they gathered their blankets and a frying-pan and other stuff.

"Lookee! This beats rabbit," said the first boy (his name was Walt); and he showed me what they had killed. It was four grouse!

Now, that was mean.

"It's against the law to kill grouse yet," I told him.

"Aw, what do we care?" he answered. "Nobody knows."

"It's only a week before the season opens, anyhow," spoke Bat. "We got the old mother and all her chickens. If we hadn't, somebody would, later."

Fellows like that are as bad as a forest fire. Just because of them, laws are made, and they break them and the rest of us keep them.

We climbed out of the gulch, and I was so mad I let them carry their own things. The woods were dusky, and I laid a straight course for camp. It was easy to find, because I knew that I had hunted with my back to it, in sound of the water on my left. All we had to do was to follow through theridge with the water on our right, and listen for voices.

I tell you, that camp looked good. The boys had two fires, a big one to dry us by and a little one to cook by. One of the tarps had been laid over a pole in crotched stakes, about four feet high, and tied down at the ends , for a dog-tent, and spruce trimmings and brush had been piled behind for a wind-break and to reflect the heat. Inside were the spruce needles that carpeted the ground and had been kept dry by branches, and a second tarp had been laid to sleep on, with the third tarp to cover us, on top of the blankets. The flags had been set up. Fitzpatrick was cooking, Major Henry was dragging more wood to burn, the fellows were drying damp stuff and stacking it safe under the panniers, or else with their feet to the big blaze were drying themselves, the burros were grazing close in. It was as light as day, with the flames reflected on the trees and the flags, and it seemed just like a trappers' bivouac.

Then we walked into the circle; and when the fellows saw the rabbits they gave a cheer. After I reported to General Ashley and turned the two boys over to him, I cleaned the rabbits for supper.

The two new boys, Bat and Walt, threw down their stuff and sat by the fire to get warm. Bat still wore his big six-shooter. They dropped their grouse in plain sight, but nobody said a word until Bat (he was the larger one) spoke up, kind of grandly, when I was finishing the rabbits:

"There's some birds. If you'll clean 'em we'll help you eat 'em."

"No, thanks. We don't want them," answered General Ashley.

"Why not?"

"It's against the law."

"Aw, what difference does that make now?" demanded Walt. "There aren't any game wardens 'round. And it's only a week before the law goes out, anyway."

"But the grouse are dead, just the same," retorted General Ashley. "They couldn't be any deader, no matter how long it is before the law opens, or if a game warden was right here!" He was getting angry, and when he's angry he isn't afraid to say anything, because he's red-headed.

"You'd like to go and tell, then; wouldn't you!" they sneered.

"I'd tell if it would do any good." And he would, too; and so would any of us. "The game laws are made to be kept. Those were our grouse and you stole them."

"Who are you?"

"Well, we happen to be a bunch of Boy Scouts. But what I mean is, that we fellows who keep the law let the game live on purpose so that everybody will have an equal chance at it, and then fellows like you come along and kill it unfairly. See?"

Humph! The two kids mumbled and kicked at the fire, as they sat; and Bat said: "We've got to have something to eat. I suppose we can cook our own meat, can't we?"

"I suppose you can," answered General Ashley, "if it'll taste good to you."

So, while Fitz was cooking on the small fire, they cleaned their own birds (I didn't touch them) and cooked over some coals of the big fire. But Fitz made bread enough for all, and there was other stuff; and the general told them to help themselves. We didn't want to be mean. The camp-fire is no place to be mean at. A mean fellow doesn't last long, out camping.

They had used bark for plates. They gave their fry-pan a hasty rub with sticks and grass, and cleaned their knives by sticking them into the ground; and then they squatted by the fire and lighted pipes. After our dishes had been washed and things had been put away for the night, and the burros picketed in fresh forage, we prepared to turn in. The clouds were low and the sky was dark, and the air was damp and chilly; so General Ashley said:

"You fellows can bunk in with us, under the tarps. We can make room."

But no! They just laughed. "Gwan," they said. "We're used to traveling light. We just roll up in a blanket wherever we happen to be. We aren't tenderfeet."

Well, we weren't, either. But we tried to be comfortable. When you are uncomfortable and sleep cold or crampy, that takes strength fighting it; and we were on the march to get that message through. So we crawled into bed, out of the wind and where the spruce branches partly sheltered us, and our tarps kept the dampness out and the wind, too. The two fellows opened their blankets (they had one apiece!) by the fire and lay down and rolled up like logs and seemed to think that they were the smarter. We let them, if they liked it so.

The wind moaned through the trees; all about us the timber was dark and lonesome. Only Apache and Sally, the burros, once in a while grunted as they stood as far inside the circle as they could get; but snuggled in our bed, low down, our heads on our coats, we were as warm as toast.

During the night I woke up, to turn over. Now and then a drop of rain hit the tarp tent. The fire was going again, and I could hear the two fellows talking. They were sitting up, feeding it, and huddled Injun fashion with their blankets over their shoulders, smoking their old pipes, and thinking (I guessed) that they were doing something big, being uncomfortable. But it takes more than such foolishness—wearing a big six-shooter when there isnothing to shoot, and sleeping out in the rain when cover is handy—to make a veteran. Veterans and real Scouts act sensibly.

When next I woke and stretched, the sun was shining and it was time to get up.

CHAPTER VI

A DISASTROUS DOZE

The two fellows were sound asleep when we turned out. They were lying in the sun, rolled up and with their faces covered to keep the light away. We didn't pay any attention to them, but had our wet rub and went ahead attending to camp duties. After a while one of them (Walt, it was) turned over, and wriggled, and threw the blanket off his face, and blinked about. He was bleary-eyed and sticky-faced, as if he had slept too hard but not long enough. And I didn't see how he had had enough air to breathe.

But he grinned, and yawned, and said: "You kids get up awful early. What time is it?"

"Six o'clock."

He-haw! And he yawned some more. Then he sat up and let his blanket go and kicked Bat. "Breakfast!" he shouted.

That made Bat grunt and grumble and wriggle; and finally uncover, too. They acted as if their mouths might taste bad, after the pipes.

We hadn't made a big fire, of course; but breakfast was about ready, on the little fire, and Fitz our cook sang out, according to our regulations: "Chuck!"

That was the camp's signal call.

"If you fellows want to eat with us, draw up and help yourselves," invited General Ashley.

"Sure," they answered; and they crawled out of their blankets, and got their pieces of bark, and opened their knives, and without washing their faces or combing their hair they fished into the dishes, for bacon and bread and sorghum and beans.

That was messy; but we wanted to be hospitable, so we didn't say anything.

"Where are you kids bound for, anyway?" asked Bat.

"Over the Divide," told General Ashley.

"Why can't we go along?"

That staggered us. They weren't our kind; and besides, we were all Boy Scouts, and our party was big enough as it was. So for a moment nobody answered. And then Walt spoke up.

"Aw, we won't hurt you any. What you afraid of? We aren't tenderfeet, and we'll do our share. We'll throw in our grub and we won't use your dishes. We've got our own outfit."

"I don't know. We'll have to vote on that," said General Ashley. "We're a Patrol of Boy Scouts, traveling on business."

"What's that—Boy Scouts?" demanded Bat.

We explained, a little.

"Take us in, then," said Walt. "We're good scouts—ain't we, Bat?"

But they weren't. They didn't know anything about Scouts and Scouts' work.

"We could admit you as recruits, on the march," said General Ashley. "But we can't swear you in."

"Aw, we'll join the gang now and you can swear us in afterwards," said Bat.

"Well," said General Ashley, doubtfully, "we'll take a vote."

We all drew off to one side, and sat in council. It seemed to me that we might as well let them in. That would be doing them a good turn, and we might help them to be clean and straight and obey the laws. Boys who seem mean as dirt, to begin with, often are turned into fine Scouts.

"Now we'll all vote just as we feel about it," said General Ashley. "One black-ball will keep them out. 'N' means 'No'; 'Y' means 'Yes.'"

The vote was taken by writing with a pencil on bits of paper, and the bits were put into General Ashley's hat. Everything was "Y"—and the vote was unanimous to let them join. So everybody must have felt the same about it as I did.

General Ashley reported to them. "You can come along," he said; "but you've got to be under discipline, the same as the rest of us. And if you prove to be Scouts' stuff you can be sworn in later. But I'm only a Patrol leader and I can't swear you."

"Sure!" they cried. "We'll be under discipline. Who's the boss? You?"

We had made a mistake. Here started our trouble. But we didn't know. We thought that we were doing the right thing by giving them a chance. You never can tell.

They volunteered to wash the dishes, and went at it; and we let them throw their blankets and whatever else they wanted to get rid of in with the packs. We were late; and anyway we didn't think it was best to start in fussing and disciplining; they would see how Scouts did, and perhaps they would catch on that way. Only—

"You'll have to cut that out," ordered General Ashley, as we were ready to set out. He meant their pipes. They had stuck them in their mouths and had lighted them.

"What? Can't we hit the pipe?" they both cried.

"Not with us," declared the general. "It's against the regulations."

"Aw, gee!" they complained. "That's the best part of camping—to load up the old pipe."

"Not for a Scout. He likes fresh air," answered General Ashley. "He needs his wind, too, and smoking takes the wind. Anyway, we're traveling through the enemy's country, and a pipe smells, and it's against Scout regulations to smoke."

They stuffed their pipes into their pockets.

"Who's the enemy?" they asked.

"We're carrying a message and some other boys are trying to stop us. That's all."

"We saw some kids, on the other side of that ridge," they cried. "They're from the same town you are. Are they the ones?"

"What did they look like?" we asked.

"One was a big kid with black eyes—" said Bat.

"Aw, he wasn't big. The big kid had blue eyes," interrupted Walt.

"How many in the party?" we asked.

"Four," said Bat.

"Five," said Walt.

"Any horses?"

"Yes."

"What were the brands?"

"We didn't notice," they said.

"Was one horse a bay with a white nose, and another a black with a bob tail?"

"Guess so," they said.

So we didn't know much more than we did before; we could only suspect. Of course, there were other parties of boys camping, in this country. We weren't the only ones. If Bat and Walt had been a little smart they might have helped us. They didn't use their eyes.

We followed the ridge we were on, as far as we could, because it was high and free from brush. General Ashley and Major Henry led, as usual, with the burros behind (those burros would follow now like dogs, where there wasn't any trail for them to pick out), and then the rest of us, the two recruits panting in the rear. Bat had belted on his big six-shooter, and Walt carried the shotgun.

We traveled fast, as usual, when we could; that gave us more time in the bad places. Pilot Peak stuck up, beyond some hills, ahead. We kept an eye on him, for he was our landmark, now that we had broken loose from trails. He didn't seem any nearer than he was the day before.

The ridge ended in a point, beyond which was a broad pasture-like meadow, with the creek winding in a semicircle through it. On across was a steep range of timber hills—and Pilot Peak and some other peaks rose beyond, with snow and rocks. In the flat a few cattle were grazing, like buffalo, and we could see an abandoned cabin which might have been a trapper's shack. It was a great scene; so free and peaceful and wild and gentle at the same time.

We weren't tired, but we halted by the stream in the flat to rest the burros and to eat something. We took off the packs, and built a little fire of dry sage, and made tea, while Sally and Apache took a good roll and then grazed on weeds and flowers and everything. This was fine, here in the sunshine, with the blue sky over and the timber sloping up on all sides, and the stream singing.

After we had eaten some bread and drunk some tea we Scouts rested, to digest; but Bat and Walt the two recruits loafed off, down the creek, and when they got away a little we could see them smoking. On top of that, they hadn't washed the dishes. So I washed them.

After a while they came back on the run, but they weren't smoking now. "Say!" they cried, excited. "We found some deer-tracks. Let's camp back on the edge of the timber, and to-night when the deer come down to drink we'll get one!"

That was as bad as shooting grouse. It wasn't deer season. They didn't seem to understand.

"Against the law," said General Ashley. "And we're on the march, to go through as quick as we can. It's time to pack."

"I'll pack one of those burros. I'll show you how," offered Bat. So we let them go ahead, because they might know more than we. They led up Sally, while Major Henry and Jed Smith and Kit Carson began to pack Apache. The recruits threw on the pack, all right, and passed the rope; but Sally moved because they were so rough, and Bat swore and kicked her in the stomach.

"Get around there!" he said.

"Here! You quit that," scolded Fitzpatrick, first. "That's no way to treat an animal." He was angry; we all were angry.

"It's the way to treat this animal," retorted Bat. "I'll kick her head off if she doesn't stand still. See?"

"No, you won't," warned General Ashley.

"If you can pack a burro so well, pack her yourself, then," answered Walt.

"Fitzpatrick, you and Jim Bridger help me with Sally," ordered the general; and we did. We threw the diamond hitch in a jiffy and the pack stuck on as if it were glued fast.

The two recruits didn't have much more to say; but when we took up the march again they sort of sulked along, behind. We thought best to follow up the creek, through the flat, instead of making a straight climb of the timber beyond. That would have been hard work, and slow work, and you can travel a mile in the open in less time than you can travel half a mile through brush.

A cattle trail led up through the flat. This flat closed, and then opened by a little pass into another flat. We saw plenty of tracks where deer had come down to the creek and had drunk. There were tracks of bucks, and of does and of fawns. Walt and Bat kept grumbling and talking. They wanted to stop off and camp, and shoot.

Pilot Peak was still on our left; but toward evening the trail we were following turned off from the creek and climbed through gooseberry and thimbleberry bushes to the top of a plateau, where was a park of cedars and flowers, and where was a spring. General Ashley dug in with his heel, and we off-packs, to camp. It was a mighty good camping spot, again. The timber thickened, beyond, and there was no sense in going on into it, for the night. Into the heel mark we stuck the flagstaff.

We went right ahead with our routine. The recruits had a chance to help, if they wanted to. But they loafed. There was plenty of time before sunset. The sun shone here half an hour or more longer than down below. We were up pretty high; some of the aspens had turned yellow, showing that there had been a frost, already. So we thought that we must be up about ten thousand feet. The stream we followed had flowed swift, telling of a steep grade.

Fitzpatrick the Bad Hand got out his camera, to take pictures. He never wasted any time. Not ordinary camp pictures, you know, but valuable pictures, of animals and sunsets and things. Jays and speckled woodpeckers were hopping about, and a pine-squirrel sat on a limb and scolded at us until he found that we were there to fit in and be company for him. One side of the plateau fell off into rocks and cliffs, and a big red ground-hog was lying out on a shelf in the sunset, and whistling his call.

Fitz was bound to have a picture of him, and sneaked around, to stalk him and snap him, close. But just as he was started—"Bang!" I jumped three feet; we all jumped. It was that fellow Bat. He had shot off his forty-five Colt's, at the squirrel, and with it smoking in his hand he was grinning, as if he had played a joke on us. He hadn't hit the squirrel, but it had disappeared. The ground-hog disappeared, the jays and the woodpeckers flew off, and after the report died away you couldn't hear a sound or see an animal. The gun had given notice to the wild life to vacate, until we were gone. And where that bullet hit, nobody could tell.

Fitzpatrick turned around and came back. He knew it wasn't much use trying, now. We were disgusted, but General Ashley was the one to speak, because he was Patrol leader.

"You ought not to do that. Shooting around camp isn't allowed," he said. "It's dangerous, and it scares things away."

"I wanted that squirrel. I almost hit him, too," answered Bat.

"Well, he was protected by camp law."

"Aw, all you kids are too fresh," put in Walt, the other. "We'll shoot as much as we please, or else we'll pull out."

"If you can't do as the rest of us do, all right: pull," answered the general.

"Let them. We don't want them," said Major Henry. "We didn't ask them in the first place. What's the sense in carrying a big revolver around, and playing tough!"

"That will do, Henry," answered the general. "I'm talking for the Patrol."

"Come on, Walt. We'll take our stuff and pull out and make our own camp," said Bat. "We won't be bossed by any red-headed kid—or any one-armed kid, either." He was referring to the gun and to the burro packing, both.

Major Henry began to sputter and growl. A black-eyed boy is as spunky as a red-headed one. And we all stood up, ready, if there was to be a fight. But there wasn't. It wasn't necessary. General Ashley flushed considerably, but he kept his temper.

"That's all right," he said. "If you can't obey discipline, like the rest, you don't camp with us."

"And we don't intend to, you bet," retorted Walt. "We're as good as you are and a little better, maybe. We're no tenderfeet!"

They gathered their blankets and their frying-pan and other outfit, and they stalked off about a hundred yards, further into the cedars, and dumped their things for their own camp.

Maybe they thought that we'd try to make them get out entirely, but we didn't own the place; it was a free camp for all, and as long as they didn't interfere with us we had no right to interfere with them. We made our fire and they started theirs; and then I was sent out to hunt for meat again.

I headed away from camp, and I got one rabbit and a great big ground-hog. Some people won't eat ground-hog, but they don't know what is good; only, he must be cleaned right away. Well, I was almost at camp again when "Whish! Bang!" somebody had shot and had spattered all around me, stinging my ear and rapping me on the coat and putting a couple of holes in my hat. I dropped flat, in a hurry.

"Hey!" I yelled. "Look out there! What you doing?"

But it was "Bang!" again, and more shot whizzing by; this time none hit me. Now I ran and sat behind a rock. And after a while I made for camp, and I was glad to reach it.

I was still some stirred up about being peppered, and so I went straight to the other fire. The two fellows were there cleaning a couple of squirrels.

"Who shot them?" I asked.

"Walt."

"And he nearly filled me full of holes, too," I said. "Look at my hat."

"Who nearly filled you full of holes?" asked Walt.

"You did."

"Aw, I didn't, either. I wasn't anywhere near you."

"You were, too," I answered, hot. "You shot right down over the hill, and when I yelled at you, you shot again."

Walt was well scared.

"'Twasn't me," he said. "I saw you start out and I went opposite."

"Well, you ought to be careful, shooting in the direction of camp," I said.

"Didn't hurt you."

"It might have put my eyes out, just the same." And I had to go back and clean my game and gun. We had a good supper. The other fellows kept to their own camp and we could smell them smoking cigarettes. With them close, and with news that another crowd was out, we were obliged to mount night guard.

There was no use in two of us staying awake at the same time, and we divided the night into four watches—eight to eleven, eleven to one, one to three, three to five. The first watch was longest, because it was the easiest watch. We drew lots for the partners who would sleep all night, and Jed Smith and Major Henry found they wouldn't have to watch. We four others would.

Fitz went on guard first, from eight to eleven. At eleven he would wake Carson, and would crawl into Carson's place beside of General Ashley. At one Carson would wake me, and would crawl into my place where I was alone. And at three I would wake General Ashley and crawl into his place beside Fitz again. So we would disturb each other just as little as possible and only at long intervals.

It seemed to me that I had the worst watch of all—from one to three; it broke my night right in two. Of course a Scout takes what duty comes, and says nothing. But jiminy, I was sleepy when Carson woke me and I had to stagger out into the dark and the cold. He cuddled down in a hurry into my warm nest and there I was, on guard over the sleeping camp, here in the timber far away from lights or houses or people.

The fire was out, but I could see by star shine. Low in the west was a half moon, just sinking behind the mountains there. Down in the flat which we had left coyotes were barking. Maybe they smelled fawns. Somebody was snoring. That was fatty Jed Smith. He and Major Henry were having a fine sleep. So were all the rest, under the whity tarps which looked ghostly and queer.

And I went to sleep, too!

That was awful, for a Scout on guard. I don't know why I couldn't keep awake, but I couldn't. I tried every way. I rubbed my eyes, and I dipped water out of the spring and washed my face, and I dropped the blanket I was wearing, so that I would be cold. And I walked in a circle. Then I thought that maybe if I sat down with the blanket about me, I would be better off. So I sat down. If I could let my eyes close for just a second, to rest them, I would be all right. And they did close—and when I opened them I was sort of toppled over against the tree, and was stiff and astonished—and it was broad morning and I hadn't wakened General Ashley!

I staggered up as quick as I could. I looked around. Things seemed to be O. K. and quiet and peaceful—but suddenly I missed the flags, and then I missed the burros!

Yes, sir! The flagstaff was gone, leaving the hole where it had been stuck. And the burros were gone, picket ropes and all! The place where they ought to be appeared mighty vacant. And now I sure was frightened. I hustled to the camp of the two boys, Bat and Walt, and they were gone. That looked bad.

My duty now was to arouse our camp and give the alarm, so I must wake General Ashley. You can imagine how I hated to. I almost was sore because he hadn't waked up, himself, at three o'clock, instead of waiting for me and letting me sleep.

But I shook him, and he sat up, blinking. I saluted. "It's after four o'clock," I reported, "and I slept on guard and the flags and the burros are gone." And then I wanted to cry, but I didn't.

CHAPTER VII

HELD BY THE ENEMY

"Oh, the dickens!" stammered General Ashley; and out he rolled, in a hurry. He didn't stop to blame me. "Have you looked for sign?"

"The burros might have strayed, but the flags couldn't and only the hole is there. And those two fellows of the other camp are gone, already."

General Ashley began to pull on his shoes and lace them.

"Rouse the camp," he ordered.

So I did. And to every one I said: "I slept on guard and the flags and the burros are gone."

I was willing to be shot, or discharged, or anything; and I didn't have a single solitary excuse. I didn't try to think one up.

The general took Fitzpatrick, who is our best trailer, and Major Henry, and started in to work out the sign, while the rest of us hustled with breakfast. The ground about the flag hole was trampled and not much could be done there; and not much could be done right where the burros had stood, because we all from both camps had been roaming around. But the general and Fitz and Major Henry circled, wider and wider, watching out for burro tracks pointing back down the trail, or else out into the timber. The hoofs of the burros would cut in, where the feet of the two fellows might not have left any mark. Pretty soon the burro tracks were found, and boot-heels, too; and while Fitzpatrick followed the trail a little farther the general and Major Henry came back to the camp. Breakfast was ready.

"Fitzpatrick and Jim Bridger and I will take the trail of the burros, and you other three stay here," said General Ashley. "If we don't come back by morning, or if you don't see smoke-signals from us that we're all right, you cache the stuff and come after us."

That was splendid of the general to give me a chance to make good on the trail. It was better than if he'd ordered me close in camp, or had not paid any attention to me.

Fitz returned, puffing. He had followed the trail a quarter of a mile and it grew plainer as the two fellows had hurried more. We ate a big breakfast (we three especially, I mean), and prepared for the trail. We tied on our coats in a roll like blankets, but we took no blankets, for we must travel light. We stuffed some bread and chocolate into our coat pockets, and we were certain that we had matches and knife. I took the short bow and arrows, as game getter; but we left the rifle for the camp. We would not have used a rifle, anyway. It made noise; and we must get the burros by Scoutcraft alone. But those burros we would have, and the flags. The general slung one of the Patrol's ropes about him, in case we had to rope the burros.

We set right out, Fitzpatrick leading, as chief trailer. Much depended upon our speed, and that is why we traveled light; for you never can follow a trail as fast as it was made, and we must overtake those fellows by traveling longer. They were handicapped by the burros, though, which helped us.

We planned to keep going, and eat on the march, and by night sneak on the camp.

The trail wasn't hard to follow. Burro tracks are different from cow tracks and horse tracks and deer tracks; they are small and oblong—narrow like a colt's hoof squeezed together or like little mule tracks. The two fellows used the cattle trail, and Fitzpatrick read the sign for us.

"They had to lead the burros," he said. "The burros' tracks are on top of the sole tracks."

We hurried. And then—

"Now they're driving 'em," he said. "They're stepping on top of the burro tracks; and I think that they're all on the trot, too, by the way the burros' hind hoofs overlap the front hoofs, and dig in."

We hurried more, at Scout pace, which is trotting and walking mixed. And next—

"Now they've got on the burros," said Fitz. "There aren't any sole tracks and the burros' hoofs dig deeper."

The fellows surely were making time. I could imagine how they kicked and licked Sally and Apache, to hasten. And while we hastened, too, we must watch the signs and be cautious that we didn't overrun or get ambushed. Where the sun shone we could tell that the sign was still an hour or more old, because the edges of the hoof-marks were baked hard; and sticks and stones turned up had dried. And in the shade the bits of needles and grass stepped on had straightened a little. And there were other signs, but we chose those which we could read the quickest.

We were high up among cedars and bushes, on a big mesa. There were cattle, here, and grassy parks for them. Most of the cattle bore a Big W brand. The trail the cattle had made kept dividing and petering out, and we had to pick the one that the burros took. The fellows were riding, still, but not at a trot so much. Maybe they thought that we had been left, by this time. Pretty soon the burros had been grabbing at branches and weeds, which showed that they were going slower, and were hungry; and the fellows had got off and were walking. The sun was high and the air was dry, so that the signs were not so easy to read, and we went slower, too. The country up here grew open and rocky, and at last we lost the trail altogether. That was bad. The general and I circled and scouted, at the sides, and Fitz went on ahead, to pick it up beyond, maybe. Pretty soon we heard him whistle the Elks' call.

He had come out upon a rocky point. The timber ended, and before and right and left was a great rolling valley, of short grasses and just a few scattered trees, with long slopes holding it like a cup. The sun was shining down, and the air was clear and quivery.

"I see them," said Fitz. "There they are, General—in a line between us and that other point of rocks."

Hurrah! This was great news. Sure enough, when we had bent low and sneaked to the rocks, and were looking, we could make out two specks creeping up the sunshine slope, among the few trees, opposite.

That was good, and it was bad. The thieves were not a mile ahead of us, then, but now we must scout in earnest. It would not do for us to keep to the trail across that open valley. Some fellows might have rushed right along; and if the other fellows were sharp they would be looking back, at such a spot, to watch for pursuers. So we must make a big circuit, and stay out of sight, and hit the trail again on the other side.

We crept back under cover, left a "warning" sign on the trail , and swung around, and one at a time we crossed the valley higher up, where it was narrower and there was brush for cover. This took time, but it was the proper scouting; and now we hurried our best along the other slope to pick up the trail once more.

It was after noon, by the sun, and we hadn't stopped to eat, and we were hungry and hot and pretty tired.

As we never talked much on the trail, especially when we might be near the enemy, Fitzpatrick made a sign that we climb straight to the top of the slope and follow along there, to strike the trail. And if the fellows had turned off anywhere, in gulch or to camp, we were better fixed above them than below them.

We scouted carefully along this ridge, and came to a gulch. A path led through, where cattle had traveled, and in the damp dirt were the burro tracks. Hurrah! They were soft and fresh.

The sun was going to set early, in a cloud bank, and those fellows would be camping soon. It was no use to rush them when they were traveling; they had guns and would hang on to the burros. The way to do was to crawl into their camp. So we traveled slower, in order to give them time to camp.

After a while we smelled smoke. The timber was thick, and the general and I each climbed a tree, to see where that smoke came from. I was away at the top of a pine, and from that tree the view was grand. Pilot Peak stood up in the wrong direction, as if we had been going around, and mountains and timber were everywhere. I saw the smoke. And away to the north, ten miles, it seemed to me I could see another smoke, with the sun showing it up. It was a column smoke, and I guessed that it was a smoke signal set by the three Scouts we had left, to show us where camp was.

But the smoke that we were after rose in a blue haze above the trees down in a little park about a quarter of a mile on our right. We left a "warning" sign, and stalked the smoke.

Although Fitzpatrick has only one whole arm, he can stalk as well as any of us. We advanced cautiously, and could smell the smoke stronger and stronger; we began to stoop and to crawl and when we had wriggled we must halt and listen. We could not hear anybody talking.

The general led, and Fitz and I crawled behind him, in a snake scout. I think that maybe we might have done better if we had stalked from three directions. Everything was very quiet, and when we could see where the fire ought to be we made scarcely a sound. The general brushed out of his way any twigs that would crack.

It was a fine stalk. We approached from behind a cedar, and parting the branches the general looked through. He beckoned to us, and we wriggled along and looked through. There was a fire, and our flags stuck beside it, and Sally and Apache standing tied to a bush, and blankets thrown down—but not anybody at home! The two fellows must be out fishing or hunting, and this seemed a good chance.

The general signed. We all were to rush in, Fitz would grab the flag, and I a burro and the general a burro, and we would skip out and travel fast, across country.

I knew that by separating and turning and other tricks we would outwit those two kids, if we got any kind of a start.

We listened, holding our breath. Nobody seemed near. Now was the time. The general stood, Fitz and I stood, and in we darted. Fitz grabbed the flag, and I was just hauling at Sally while the general slashed the picket-ropes with his knife, when there rose a tremendous yell and laugh and from all about people charged in on us.

Before we could escape we were seized. They were eight to our three. Two of them were the two kids Bat and Walt, and the other six were town fellows—Bill Duane, Tony Matthews, Bert Hawley, Mike Delavan, and a couple more.

How they whooped! We felt cheap. The camp had been a trap. The two kids Bat and Walt had come upon the other crowd accidentally, and had told about us and that maybe we were trailing them, and they all had ambushed us. We ought to have reconnoitered more, instead of thinking about stalking. We ought to have been more suspicious, and not have underestimated the enemy. This was just a made-to-order camp. The camp of the town gang was about three hundred yards away, lower, in another open place, by a creek. They tied our arms and led us down there.

"Aw, we thought you fellers were Scouts!" jeered Bat. "You're easy."

He and Walt took the credit right to themselves.

"What do you want with us?" demanded General Ashley, of Bill Duane. "We haven't done anything to harm you."

"We'll show you," said Bill. "First we're going to skin you, and then we're going to burn you at the stake, and then we're going to kill you."

Of course we knew that he was only fooling; but it was a bad fix, just the same. They might keep us, for meanness; and Major Henry and Kit Carson and Jed Smith wouldn't know exactly what to do and we'd be wasting valuable time. That was the worst: we were delaying the message! And I had myself to blame for this, because I went to sleep on guard. A little mistake may lead to a lot of trouble.

And now the worst happened. When they got us to the main camp Bill Duane walked up to General Ashley and said: "Where you got that message, Red?"

"What message?" answered General Ashley.

"Aw, get out!" laughed Bill. "If we untie you will you fork it over or do you want me to search you?"

"'Tisn't your message, and if I had it I wouldn't give it to you. But you'd better untie us, just the same. And we want those burros and our flags."

"Hold him till I search him, fellows," said Bill. "He's got it, I bet. He's the Big Scout."

Fitz and I couldn't do a thing. One of the gang put his arm under the general's chin and held him tight, and Bill Duane went through him. He didn't find the message in any pockets; but he saw the buckskin thong, and hauled on it, and out came the packet from under the general's shirt.

Bill put it in his own pocket.

"There!" he said. "Now what you going to do about it?"

The general was as red all over as his hair and looked as if he wanted to fight or cry. Fitz was white and red in spots, and I was so mad I shook.

"Nothing, now," said the general, huskily. "You don't give us a chance to do anything. You're a lot of cowards—tying us up and searching us, and taking our things."

"BILL DUANE WENT THROUGH HIM."

Then they laughed at us some more, and all jeered and made fun, and said that they would take the message through for us. I tell you, it was humiliating, to be bound that way, as prisoners, and to think that we had failed in our trust. As Scouts we had been no good — and I was to blame just because I had fallen asleep at my post.

They were beginning to quit laughing at us, and were starting to get supper, when suddenly I heard horse's hoofs, and down the bridle path that led along an edge of the park rode a man. He heard the noise and he saw us tied, I guess, for he came over.

"What's the matter here?" he asked.

The gang calmed down in a twinkling. They weren't so brash, now.

"Nothin'," said Bill.

"Who you got here? What's the rumpus?" he insisted.

"They've taken us prisoners and are keeping us, and they've got our burros and flags and a message," spoke up the general.

He was a small man with a black mustache and blackish whiskers growing. He rode a bay horse with a K Cross on its right shoulder, and the saddle had brass-bound stirrups. He wore a black slouch hat and was in black shirt-sleeves, and ordinary pants and shoes.

"What message?" he asked.

"A message we were carrying."

"Where?"

"Across from our town to Green Valley."

"Why?"

"Just for fun."

"Aw, that's a lie. They were to get twenty-five dollars for doing it on time. Now we cash it in ourselves," spoke Bill. "It was a race, and they don't make good. See?"

That was a lie, sure. We weren't to be paid a cent—and we didn't want to be paid.

"Who's got the message now?" asked the man.

"He has," said the general, pointing at Bill.

"Let's see it."

Bill backed away.

"I ain't, either," he said. Which was another lie.

"Let's see it," repeated the man. "I might like to make that twenty-five dollars myself."

Now Bill was sorry he had told that first lie. The first is the one that gives the most trouble.

"Who are you?" he said, scared, and backing away some more.

"Never you mind who I am," answered the man—biting his words off short; and he rode right for Bill. He stuck his face forward. It was hard and dark and mean. "Hand—over—that—message. Savvy?"

Bill was nothing but a big bluff and a coward. You would have known that he was a coward, by the lies he had told and by the way he had attacked us. He wilted right down.

"Aw, I was just fooling," he said. "I was going to give it back to 'em. Here 'tis. There ain't no prize offered, anyhow." And he handed it to the man.

The man turned it over in his fingers. We watched. We hoped he'd make them untie us and he'd pass it to us and tell us to skip. But after he had turned it over and over, he smiled, kind of grimly, and stuck it in his hip pocket.

"I reckon I'd like to make that twenty-five dollars myself," he said. And then he rode to one side, and dismounted; he loosened the cinches and made ready as if to camp. And they all let him.

Now, that was bad for us, again. The gang had our flags and our burros, and he had our message.

"That's our message. We're carrying it through just for fun and for practice," called the general. "It's no good to anybody except us."

"Bueno," said the man—which is Mexican or Spanish for "Good." He was squatting and building a little fire.

"Aren't you going to give it to us and make them let us go?"

He grunted. "Don't bother me. I'm busy."

That was all we could get out of him. Now it was growing dark and cold. The gang was grumbling and accusing Bill of being "bluffed" and all that, but they didn't make any effort to attack the man. They all were afraid of him; they didn't have nerve. They just grumbled and talked of what Bill ought to have done, and proceeded to cook supper and to loaf around. Our hands were behind our backs and we were tied like dogs to trees.

And suddenly, while watching the man, I noticed that he was doing things left-handed, and quick as a wink I saw that the sole of his left shoe was worn through! And if he wasn't riding a roan horse, he was riding a saddle with brass-bound stirrups, anyway. A man may trade horses, but he keeps to his own saddle. This was the beaver man! We three Scouts exchanged signs of warning.

"You aren't going to tie us for all night, are you?" demanded Fitzpatrick.

"Sure," said Bill.

"We'll give you our parole not to try to escape," offered General Ashley.

"What's that?"

"We'll promise," I explained.

Then they all jeered.

"Aw, promise!" they laughed. "We know all about your promises."

"Scouts don't break their promises," answered the general, hot. "When we give our parole we mean it. And if we decided to try to escape we'd tell you and take the parole back. We want to be untied so we can eat."

"All right. We'll untie you," said Bill; and I saw him wink at the other fellows.

They did. They loosened our hands—but they put ropes on our feet! We could just walk, and that is all. And Walt (he and Bat were cooking) poked the fire with our flagstaff. Then he sat on the flags! I tell you, we were angry!

"This doesn't count," sputtered the general, red as fury.

"You gave us your parole if we'd untie you," jeered Bill. "And we did."

"But you tied us up again."

"We didn't say anything about that. You said if we'd untie you, so you could eat, you wouldn't run away. Well, we untied you, didn't we?"

"That isn't fair. You know what we meant," retorted Fitz.

"We know what you said," they laughed.

"Aw, cut it out," growled the man, from his own fire. "You make too much noise. I'm tired."

"Chuck," called Walt, for supper.

They stuck us between them, and we all ate. Whew, but it was a dirty camp. The dishes weren't clean and the stuff to eat was messy, and the fellows all swore and talked as bad as they could. It was a shame—and it seemed a bigger shame because here in the park everything was intended to be quiet and neat and ought to make you feel good.

After supper they quarreled as to who would wash the dishes, and finally one washed and one wiped, and the rest lay around and smoked pipes and cigarettes. Over at his side of the little park the man had rolled up and was still. But I knew that he was watching, because he was smoking, too.

We couldn't do anything, even if we had planned to. We might have untied the ropes on our feet, but the gang sat close about us. Then, they had the flags and the burros, and the man had the message; and if they had been wise they would have known that we wouldn't go far. Of course, we might have hung about and bothered them.

They made each of us sleep with one of them. They had some dirty old quilts, and we all rolled up.

CHAPTER VIII

A NEW USE FOR A CAMERA

We were stiff when we woke in the morning, but we had to lie until the rest of them decided to get up, and then it was hot and late. That was a lazy camp as well as a dirty one. The early morning is the best part of the day, out in the woods, but lots of fellows don't seem to think so.

I had slept with Bat, and he had snored 'most all night. Now as soon as I could raise my head from the old quilts I looked over to see the man. He wasn't there. His horse wasn't there and his fire wasn't burning. The spot where he had camped was vacant. He had gone, with our message!

I wriggled loose from Bat and woke him, and he swore and tried to make me lie still, but I wouldn't. Not much!

"Red!" I called, not caring whether I woke anybody else or not. "Red! General!" I used both names—and I didn't care for that, either.

He wriggled, too, to sit up.

"What?"

"The man's gone. He isn't there. He's gone with the message!"

The general exclaimed, and worked to jerk loose from Bill; and Fitz's head bobbed up. There wasn't any more sleep for that camp, now.

"Oh, shut up!" growled Bill.

"You fellows turn us loose," we ordered. "We've got to go. We've got to follow that man."

But they wouldn't, of course. They just laughed, and said: "No, you don't want to go. You've given us your parole; see?" and they pulled us down into the quilts again, and yawned and would sleep some more, until they found it was no use, and first one and then another kicked off the covers and sat up, too.

The sun was high and all the birds and bees and squirrels were busy for the day. At least two hours had been wasted, already.

Half of the fellows didn't wash at all, and all we Scouts were allowed to do was to wash our faces, with a lick and a promise, at the creek, under guard. We missed our morning cold wet rub. The camp hadn't been policed, and seemed dirtier than ever. Tin cans were scattered about, and pieces of bacon and of other stuff, and there was nothing sanitary or regular. Our flags were dusty and wrinkled; and that hurt. The only thing homelike was Apache and Sally, our burros, grazing on weeds and grass near the camp. But they didn't notice us particularly.

We didn't have anything more to say. The fellows began to smoke cigarettes and pipes as soon as they were up, and made the fire and cooked some bacon and fried some potatoes, and we all ate, with the flies buzzing around. A dirty camp attracts flies, and the flies stepped in all sorts of stuff and then stepped in our food and on us, too. Whew! Ugh!

We would have liked to make a smoke signal, to let Major Henry and Jed Smith and Kit Carson know where we were, but there seemed no way. They would be starting out after us, according to instructions, and we didn't want them to be captured. We knew that they would be coming, because they were Scouts and Scouts obey orders. They can be depended upon.

I guess it was ten o'clock before we were through the messy breakfast, and then most of the gang went off fishing and fooling around.

"Aren't you going to untie our feet?" asked the general.

"Do you give us your promise not to skip?" answered Bill.

"We'll give our parole till twelve o'clock."

We knew what the general was planning. By twelve o'clock something might happen — the other Scouts might be near, then, and we wanted to be free to help them. —

"Will you give us your parole if we tie your feet, loose, instead of your hands?"

"Yes," said the general; and Fitzpatrick and I nodded. Jiminy, we didn't want our hands tied, on this hot day.

So they hobbled our feet, and tethered us to a tree. They tied the knots tight—knot after knot; and then they went off laughing, but they left Walt and Bat to watch us! That wasn't fair. It broke our parole for us, really, for they hadn't accepted it under the conditions we had offered it.

"Don't you fellows get to monkeying, now," warned Bat, "or we'll tie you tighter. If you skip we've got your burros and your flags."

That was so.

"We know that," replied the general, meekly; but I could see that he was boiling, inside.

It was awful stupid, just sitting, with those two fellows watching. Bat wore his big revolver, and Walt had his shotgun. They smoked their bad-smelling pipes, and played with an old deck of cards. Camping doesn't seem to amount to much with some fellows, except as a place to be dirty in and to smoke and play cards. They might as well be in town.

"Shall we escape?" I signed to the general.

"No," he signed back. "Wait till twelve o'clock." He was going to keep our word, even if we did have a right to break it.

"Hand me my camera, will you, please?" asked Fitz, politely.

"What do you want of it?" demanded Walt.

"I want to use it. We haven't anything else to do."

"Sure," said Walt; he tossed it over. "Take pictures of yourselves, and show folks how you smart Scouts were fooled."

I didn't see what Fitz could use his camera on, here. And he didn't seem to be using it. He kept it beside him, was all. There weren't any animals around this kind of a camp. But the general and I didn't ask him any questions. He was wise, was old Fitzpatrick the Bad Hand, and probably he had some scheme up his sleeve.

We just sat. The two fellows played cards and smoked and talked rough and loud, and wasted their time this way. The sun was mighty hot, and they yawned and yawned. Tobacco smoking so much made them stupid. But we yawned, too. The general made the sleep sign to Fitz and me, and we nodded. The general and I stretched out and were quiet. I really was sleepy; we had had a hard night.

"You fellows going to sleep?" asked Walt.

We grunted at him.

"Then we'll tie your hands and we'll go to sleep," he said. "Come on, Bat. Maybe it's a put-up job."

"No, sir; that wasn't in the bargain," objected the general.

"Aw, we got your parole till twelve o'clock, but we're going to tie you anyway," replied that Walt. "We didn't say how long we'd leave your hands loose. We aren't going to sit around and keep awake, watching you guys. When we wake up we untie you again."

We couldn't do anything; and they tied the general's hands and my hands, but Fitzpatrick begged off.

"I want to use my camera," he claimed. "And I've got only one hand anyway. I can't untie knots with one hand."

They didn't know how clever Fitz was; so they just moved him and fastened him by the waist to a tree where he couldn't reach us.

"We'll be watching and listening," they warned. "And if you try any foolishness you'll get hurt."

They stretched out, and pretended to snooze. I didn't see, myself, how Fitz could untie those hard knots with his one hand, in time to do any good. They were hard knots, drawn tight, and the rope was a clothes-line; and he was set against a tree with the rope about his body and the knots behind him on the other side of the tree. I didn't believe that Bat and Walt would sleep hard; but while I waited to see what would happen next, I dozed off, myself.

Something tapped me on the head, and I woke up in a jiffy. Fitz must have tossed a twig at me, because when I looked over at him he made the silence sign. He was busy; and what do you think? He had taken his camera apart, and unscrewed the lenses, and had focused on the rope about him. He had wriggled so that the sun shone on the lenses, and a little spire of smoke was rising from him. Bat and Walt were asleep; they never made a move, but they both snored. And Fitz was burning his rope in two, on his body.

It didn't take very long, because the sun was so hot and the lenses were strong. The rope charred and fumed, and he snapped it; and then he began on his feet. Good old Fitz! If only he got loose before those two fellows woke. The general was watching him, too.

Walt grunted and rolled over and bleared around, and Fitz quit instantly, and sat still as if tied and fooling with his camera. Walt thought that everything was all right and rolled over; and after a moment Fitz continued. Pretty soon he was through. And now came the most ticklish time of all.

He waited and made a false move or two, to be certain that Walt and Bat weren't shamming; and then he snapped the rope about his body and gradually unwound it and then he snapped the rope that bound together his feet. Now he began to crawl for the two fellows. Inch by inch he moved along, like an Indian; and he never made a sound. That was good scouting for anybody, and especially for a one-armed boy, I tell you! The general and I scarcely breathed. My heart thumped so that I was afraid it would shake the ground.

When he got near enough, Fitz reached cautiously, and pulled away the shotgun. Like lightning he opened the breech and shook loose the shell and kicked it out of the way—and when he closed the breech with a jerk Bat woke up.

"You keep quiet," snapped Fitz. His eyes were blazing. "If either of you makes a fuss, I'll pull the trigger." He had the gun aiming straight at them both. Walt woke, too, and was trying to discover what happened. "Be quiet, now!"

Those two fellows were frightened stiff. The gun looked ugly, with its round muzzle leveled at their stomachs, and Fitz behind, his cheeks red and his eyes angry and steady. But it was funny, too; he might have pulled trigger, but nothing would have happened, because the gun wasn't loaded. Of course none of us Scouts would have shot anybody and had blood on our hands. Fitz had thrown away the shell on purpose so that there wouldn't be any accident. It's bad to point a gun, whether loaded or not, at any one. This was a have-to case. Bat and Walt didn't know. They were white as sheets, and lay rigid.

"Don't you shoot. Look out! That gun might go off," they pleaded; we could hear their teeth chatter. "If you won't point it at us we'll do anything you say."

"You bet you'll do anything I say," snapped Fitz, very savage. "You had us, and now we have you! Unbuckle that belt, you Bat. Don't you touch the revolver, though. I'm mad and I mean business."

Bat's fingers trembled and he fussed at the belt and unbuckled it, and off came belt and revolver, and all.

"Toss 'em over."

He tossed them. Fitz put his foot on them.

"Aw, what do you let that one-armed kid bluff you for?" began Walt; and Fitz caught him up as quick as a wink.

"What are you talking about?" he asked. "I'll give you a job, too. You take your knife and help cut those two Scouts loose."

"Ain't got a knife," grumbled Walt.

"Yes, you have. I've seen it. Will you, or do you want me to pull trigger?"

"You wouldn't dare."

"Wouldn't I? You watch this finger."

"Look out, Walt!" begged Bat. "He will! I know he will! See his finger? He might do it by accident. Quit, Fitz. We'll cut 'em."

"Don't get up. Just roll," ordered Fitz.

They rolled. He kept the muzzle right on them. Walt cut me free (his hands were shaking as bad as Bat's), and Bat cut the general free.

We stood up. But there wasn't time for congratulations, or anything like that. No. We must skip.

"Quick!" bade Fitz. "Tie their feet. My rope will do; it was a long one."

"How'd you get loose?" snarled Walt.

"None of your business," retorted Fitz.

We pulled on the knots hard—and they weren't any granny knots, either, that would work loose. We tied their feet, and then with a bowline noose tied their elbows behind their backs—which was quicker than tying their wrists.

Fitz dropped the shotgun and grabbed his camera.

"You gave your parole," whined Bat.

"It's after twelve," answered the general.

And then Walt uttered a tremendous yell—and there was an answering whoop near at hand. The rest of the gang were coming back.

"Run!" ordered the general. "Meet at the old camp."

We ran, and scattered. We didn't stop for the burros, or anything more, except that as I passed I grabbed up the bow and arrows and with one jerk I ripped our flags loose from the pole, where it was lying.

This delayed me for a second. Walt and Bat were yelling the alarm, and feet were hurrying and voices were answering. I caught a glimpse of the general and Fitz plunging into brush at one side, and I made for another point.

"There they go! Stop 'em!" were calling Walt and Bat.

Tony Matthews was coming so fast that he almost dived into me; but I dodged him and away I went, into the timber and the brush, with him pelting after. Now all the timber was full of cries and threats, and "Bang! Bang!" sounded a gun. But I didn't stop to look around. I scudded, with Tony thumping behind me.

"You halt!" ordered Tony. "Head him off!" he called.

I dodged again, around a cedar, and ran in a new direction, up a slope, through grass and just a sprinkling of trees. Now was the time to prove what a Scout's training was good for, in giving him lungs and legs and endurance. So I ran at a springy lope, up-hill, as a rabbit does. Two voices were panting at me; I saved my breath for something better than talk. The puffing grew fainter, and finally when I couldn't hear it, or any other sound near, I did halt and look around.

The pursuit was still going on behind and below, near where the gang's camp was. I could hear the shouts, and "Bang! Bang!" but shouts and shooting wouldn't capture the general and Fitz, I knew. Tony and the other fellow who had been chasing me had quit—and now I saw the general and Fitz. They must have had to double and dodge, because they had not got so far away: but here they came, out from the trees, into an open space, across from me, and they were running strong and swift for the slope beyond. If it was a case of speed and wind, none of that smoking, flabby crowd could catch them.

Fitz was ahead, the general was about ten feet behind, and much farther behind streamed the gang, Bill Delaney leading and the rest lumbering after. Tony and the other fellow had flopped down, and never stirred to help. They were done for.

It was quite exciting, to watch; and as the general and Fitz were drawing right away and escaping, I wanted to cheer. They turned sharp to make straight up-hill—and then the general fell. He must have slipped. He picked himself up almost before he had touched the ground and plunged on, but down he toppled, like a wounded deer. Fitzpatrick, who was climbing fast off at one side, saw.

"Hurt?" I heard him call.

"No," answered the general. "Go on."

But Fitz didn't keep on. He turned and came right to him, although the enemy was drawing close. The general staggered up, and sat down again.

I knew what was being said, now, although I couldn't hear anything except the jeers of the gang as they increased speed. The general was hurt, and he was telling Fitz to go and save himself, and Fitz wouldn't. He sat there, too, and waited. Then, just as the gang closed in, and Bill Delaney reached to grab Fitz, the general saw me and made me the sign to go on, and the sign of a horse and rider.

Yes, that was my part, now. I was the one who must follow the beaver man, who had taken our message. The message was the most important thing. We must get that through no matter what happened. And while Fitz and the general could help each other, inside, I could be trailing the message, and maybe finding Henry and Carson and Smith, outside.

So I started on. The enemy was leading the general, who could just hobble, and Fitz, back to the camp. Loyal old Fitzpatrick the Bad Hand, who had helped his comrade instead of saving himself!

CHAPTER IX

JIM BRIDGER ON THE TRAIL

I turned, and climbed the hill. It was a long hill, and hot, but I wanted to get up where I could see. The top was grassy and bare, and here I stopped, to find out where things were.

Off in one direction (which was southwest, by the sun) rose Pilot Peak, rocky and snowy, with the main range stretching on either side of it. But between Pilot Peak and me there lay a big country of heavy timber. Yes, in every direction was heavy timber. I had run without thinking, and now it was pretty hard to tell exactly where I was.

I stood for a minute and tried to figure in what direction that beaver man probably had ridden. He had come in on our left, as we sat, and had probably gone along toward our right. I tried to remember which way the shadows had fallen, in the sunset, and which way west had been, from our right or left as we were sitting.

Finally I was quite certain that the shadows had fallen sort of quartering, from right to left, and so the man probably had made toward the west. It was a good thing that I had noticed the shadows, but to notice little things is a Scout's training.

I stuffed the flags inside my shirt, and tied my coat about me; only one arrow was left, out of six; the five others must have fallen when I was running. And I was hungry and didn't have a thing to eat, because when the gang had captured us they had taken our bread and chocolate, along with our match-boxes and knives and other stuff. That was mean of them. But with a look about for smoke signals I took my bow and started across the top of the hill.

It was to be the lone trail and the hungry trail for Jim Bridger. But he had slept on post, and he was paying for it. Now if he (that was I, you know) only could get back that message, and thus make good, he wouldn't mind lonesomeness or hunger or thirst or tiredness or wet or anything.

I wasn't afraid of the gang overtaking me or finding me, if I kept my wits about me. And after I was over the brow of the hill I swung into the west, at Scouts' pace of trot and walk mixed. This took me along the top of the hill, to a draw or little valley that cut through. The draw was thick with spruces and pines and was brushy at the bottom, so I went around the head of it. That was easier than climbing down and up again—and the draw would have been a bad place to be cornered in.

I watched out for trails, but I did not cross a thing, and I began to edge down to strike that stream which passed the gang's camp. Often trails follow along streams, where the cattle and horses travel. The man who had our message might have used this trail but although I edged and edged, keeping right according to the sun, I didn't strike that stream. Up and down and up again, through the trees and through the open places I toiled and sweated; and every time I came out upon a ridge, expecting to be at the top of somewhere, another ridge waited; and every time I reached the bottom of a draw or gulch, expecting that here was my stream or a trail, or both, I found that I was fooled again.

This up and down country covered by timber is a mighty easy country to be lost in. I wasn't lost—the stream was lost. No, I wasn't lost; but when I came out upon a rocky ridge, and climbed to the top of a bunch of granite there, the world was all turned around. Pilot Peak had changed shape and was behind me when it ought to have been before. West was west, because the sun was setting in it, but it seemed queer. You see, I had been zigzagging about to make easy climbs out of draws and gulches, and to dodge rocks and brush—and here I was.

You may believe that now I was mighty hungry and thirsty, and I was tired, too. This was a fine place to see from, and I sat on a ledge and looked about, mapping the country. That was Pilot Peak, away off on the left; and that was the Medicine Range, on either side of it. It was the range that we Scouts must cross, if ever we got to it. But between me and the range lay miles of rolling timber, and all about below me lay the timber, with here and there bare rocky points sticking up like the tips of breakers in an ocean and here and there little winding valleys, like the oily streaks in the ocean. Away off in one valley seemed to be a cleared field where grain had been cut; but no ranch house was there. It was just a patch. In all this big country I was the only inhabitant—I and the wild things.

Well, I must camp for the night. The sun was setting behind the mountains. If I tried traveling blind by night I might get all tangled up in the timber and brush and be in a bad fix. Up here it was dry and open and the rocks would shelter me from the wind. I tried to be calm and reasonable and use Scout sense; and I decided to stay right where I was, till morning.

But jiminy, I was hungry and thirsty, and I wanted a fire, too. This was pretty good experience, to be lost without food or drink or matches, or even a knife—it was pretty good experience if I managed right.

There were plenty of dead dried branches scattered here among the rocks, and pack-rats had made a nest of firewood. But first, as seemed to me, I must get a drink and something for supper. I had only that one arrow to depend on, for game, and if I waited much longer then I might lose it in the dusk. Not an easy shot had shown itself, either, during all the time I had been traveling.

Water was liable to be down there somewhere, in those valleys, and I looked to see which was the greenest or which had any willows. To the greenest it seemed a long way. Then I had a clue. I saw a flock of grouse. They sailed out from the timber and across and slanted down into a gulch. More followed. They acted as if they were bound somewhere on purpose, and I remembered that grouse usually drink before they go to bed.

These were so far away, below me, that I couldn't make out whether they were sage grouse, or the blue grouse, or the fool grouse. If they were sage grouse, I might not get near enough to them to shoot sure with my one arrow. If they were blue grouse, that would be bad, too, for blue grouse are sharp. If they were fool grouse, I ought to get one. I marked exactly where they sailed for, and down I went, keeping my eye on the spot. Now I must use Scoutcraft for water and food. If I couldn't manage a fire, I could chew meat raw.

Yes, I remembered that it was against the law to kill grouse, yet. I thought about it a minute; and decided that the law did not intend that a starving person should not kill just enough for meat when he had nothing else. I was willing to tell the first ranger or game warden, and pay a fine—but I must eat. And I hoped that what I was trying to do was all right. Motives count, in law, don't they?

Down I went, as fast as I could go. The sun was just sinking out of sight. It was the lonesome time of day for a fellow without fire or food or shelter, in the places where nobody lived, and I wouldn't have objected much if I'd been home at the supper table.

I reached the bottom of the hill. It ended at the edge of some aspens. Their white trunks were ghostly in the twilight. Across through the aspens I hurried, straight as I could go; and I came out into a grassy, boggy place—a basin where water from the hills around was seeping! Hurrah! It was a regular spring, and the water ran trickling away, down through a gulch.

Grasses grew high: wild timothy and wild oats and gama grass, mingled with flowers. Along the trickle were willows, too. With the aspens and the willows and the seed grasses and the water this was a fine place for grouse. I looked for sign, on the edge of the wetness, and I saw where birds had been scratching and taking dust baths, in a patch of sage.

Stepping slowly, and keeping sharp lookout, I reconnoitered about the place; I was so excited that I didn't stop to drink. And suddenly—whirr-rr-rr! With a tremendous noise up flew two grouse, and three more, and lit in the willows right before me. I guess I was nervous, I wanted them so bad; for I jumped back and stumbled and fell, and broke the arrow square in two with my knee.

That made me sick. Here was my supper waiting for me, and I had spoiled my chances. I wanted to cry.

Those acted like fool grouse. They sat with their heads and necks stretched, watching me and everything else. I picked up the two pieces of my arrow; and then I looked about for a straight reed or willow twig that might do. Something rustled right before me, and there was another grouse! It had been sitting near enough to bite me and I hadn't seen it.

By the feathers I knew it was a fool grouse. Was it going to fly, or not? I stood perfectly still, and then I squatted gradually and gave it time. After it had waggled its head around, it moved a little and began to peck and cackle; and I could hear other cackles answering. If I only could creep near enough to hit it with a stick.

I reached a dead willow stick, and squatting as I was I hitched forward, inch by inch. Whenever the grouse raised its silly head I scarcely breathed.The grass was clumpy, and once behind a clump I wriggled forward faster. With the clump between me and the grouse I approached as close as I dared. The grouse was only four or five feet away. It must be now or never, for when once the grouse began to fly for their night's roost mine would go, too.

Fool grouse you can knock off of limbs with a stone, or with a club when they are low enough and when they happen to be feeling in the mood to be knocked. Behind my clump I braced my toes, and out I sprang and swiped hard, but the grouse fluttered up, just the same, squawking. I hit again, hard and quick, and struck it down, and I pounced on it and had it! Yes, sir, I had it! All around me grouse were flying and whirring off, and those in the tree joined them; but I didn't care now.

I lay on my stomach and took a long drink of water, and back I hustled for camp.

Down here the dark had gathered; but up on the hill the light stayed, and of course the top of the hill, where my camp was, would be light longest. Now if I only could manage a fire. I had an idea—a good Scout idea.

First I picked out a place for the night. In one spot the faces of two rocks met at an angle. The grass here was dead and softish, and the wind blowing off the snowy range on the west didn't get in. I gathered a bunch of the grass, and tore my handkerchief with my teeth and mixed some ravelings of that in and tied a nest, with a handle to it. Then I got some of the dry twigs lying about, and had them ready. Then I found a piece of flinty rock—I think it was quartzite; and I took off a shoe and struck the rock on the hob nails, over the nest of grass.

It worked! The sparks flew and landed in the loose knot, and I blew to start them. After I had been trying, I saw a little smoke, and smelled it; and so I grabbed the nest by its handle and swung it. It caught fire, and in a jiffy I had it on the ground, with twigs across it—and I was fixed. A fire makes a big difference. I wasn't lonesome any more. This camp was home.

I was so hungry that I didn't more than half cook the grouse by holding pieces on a stick over the blaze, trapper style. While I gnawed I went out around the rocks and watched the sunset. It was glorious, and the pink and gold lasted, with the snowy range and old Pilot Peak showing sharp and cold against it. Up here I was right in the twilight, while below the timber and the valleys were dark.

I must collect wood while I could see, beginning with the pieces furthest away. Down at the bottom of the hill I had marked a big branch; and out I hiked and hauled it up. That camp looked grand when I came in again; the bottom of the hill was gloomy, but here I had a fire.

The sunset was done; everything was dark; the stars were shining all through the sky; from the timber below queer cries and calls floated up to me, but there was nothing to be afraid of. I was minding my business, and animals would be minding theirs. So I moved the fire forward a little from the angle of the rocks, and sat in the angle myself. Wow, but it was warm and nice! I couldn't make a big fire, because I didn't want to run out of fuel; but the little fire was better, as long as it was large enough to be cheerful and to warm me. I spliced my broken arrow with string.

This was real Scout coziness. Of course, I sort of wished that Fitz or little Jed Smith or somebody else was there, for company; but I'd done pretty well. I tried to study the stars—but as I sat I kept nodding and dozing off, and waking with a jerk, and so I pulled the thick part of the branch across the fire and shoved in the scattered ends. Then I wrapped the flags about my neck and over my head, and sitting flat with my back against the rock I went to sleep. Indians say that they keep warm best by covering their shoulders and head, even if they can't cover their legs.

Something woke me with a start. I lay shivering and listening. The fire flickered low, the sky was close above me, darkness was around about, and behind me was a rustle, rustle, patter, patter. At first I was silly and frightened; but with a jump I quit that and ordered, loud:

"Get out of there!"

Wild animals are especially afraid of the human voice; and whatever this was it scampered away. Then I decided that it was only a pack-rat. Anyhow, there would be nothing out here in these hills to attack a human being while he slept. Even the smell of a human being will keep most animals off. They're suspicious of him. And I thought of the hundreds of old-time trappers and hunters, and of the prospectors and ranchers and range-riders, who had slept right out in the timber, in a blanket, and who never had been molested at all. So I didn't reckon that anything was going to climb this hill to get me!

I stirred about and built the fire, and got warm. The Guardians of the Pole had moved around a quarter of the clock, at least, and the moon was away over in the west, so I knew that I must have slept quite a while.

The night was very quiet. Here on the hill I felt like a Robinson Crusoe marooned on his island. I stood and peered about; everywhere below was the dark timber; the moon was about to set behind the snowy range; overhead were the stars—thousands of them in a black sky, which curved down on all sides.

The Milky Way was plain. The Indians say that is the trail the dead warriors take to the Happy Hunting Grounds. I could see the North Star, of course, and I could see the Papoose on the Squaw's back, in the handle of the Great Dipper; so I had Scout's eyesight. In the west was the evening star — Jupiter, I guessed. Off south was the Scorpion, and the big red star Antares. I wished that the Lost Children were dancing in the sky, but they had not come yet.

It made me calm, to get out this way and look at the stars. I'd been lucky, so far, to have fire and supper and a good camp, and I decided that I would get that message — or help get it. Somewhere down in that world of timber were Major Henry and Kit Carson and little Jed Smith, on the trail; and General Ashley and wise Fitzpatrick the Bad Hand, planning to escape; and the man who had the message. And here was I, on detail that seemed to have happened, and yet seemed to have been ordered, too. And watchful and steady as the stars, above us was the Great Commander, who knew just how things would come out, here in the hills the same as in the cities. It's kind of comforting, when a fellow realizes that he can't get lost entirely, and that Somebody knows where he is and what he is doing, and what he wants to do.

In the morning I would strike off southwest, and keep going until I came to a trail where the beaver man had traveled, or until I had some sight of him or news of him.

By the Pointers it was midnight. So after thinking things over I fed the fire and warmed my back; then I hunched into the angle and with the two flags about my shoulders and over my head I started to snooze off. Some animal kept rustling and pattering, but I let it rustle and patter.

Just as I was snoozing, I remembered that to-morrow — that to-day was Sunday! Yes; I counted, and we had left town on Monday and we had been out six days. I supposed that I ought to rest on Sunday; but I didn't see how I could, fixed as I was; and I hoped that if I took the trail I would be understood.

CHAPTER X

THE RED FOX PATROL

When I woke up I was safe and sound, but I had thrown off the flags and I was stiff and cold. Now I could see all about me—see the rocks and the grass and the ashes of the fire; so morning had come. That was good.

After I had yawned and stretched and straightened out, I gave a little dance to start my circulation. Then I built the fire from the coals that were left, and cooked the rest of the grouse, and had breakfast, chewing well so as to get all the nourishment that I could. I climbed on a rock, in the sun, like a ground-hog, to eat, and to look about at the same time. And I saw smoke!

The smoke was lifting above the timber away off, below. This was a fine morning; a Sunday morning, peaceful and calm, and the smoke rose in a little curl, as if it were from a camp or a chimney. I took that as a good omen. Down I sprang, to my own fire; and heaped on damp stuff and dirt, and using my coat made the private smoke signal of the Elk Patrol: one puff, three puffs, and one puff. But the other smoke didn't answer.

Then I thought of making the signal meaning "I am lost. Help"; but I said to myself: "No, you don't. You're not calling for help, yet. You'd be a weak kind of a Scout, to sit down and call for help. There's a sign for you. Maybe that smoke is the beaver man. Sic him." And trampling out my own fire, and stuffing the flags into my shirt and tying my jacket around me, lining that other fire by a dead pine at the foot of the hill, away I went.

When I got to the dead pine I drew another bee-line ahead as far as I could see, with a stump as the end, and followed that. But this was an awful rough, thick country. First I got into a mess of fallen timber, where the dead trunks were criss-crossed like jackstraws; and they were smooth and hard and slippery, and I had to climb over and crawl under and straddle and slide, and turn back several times, and I lost my bee-line. But I set my direction again by the sun on my face. Next I ran into a stretch of those small black-jacks, so thick I could scarcely squeeze between. And when I came out I was hot and tired, I tell you!

Now I was hungry, too, and thirsty; and I found that fire meant a whole lot to me. If it didn't mean the man with the message, it meant food and somebody to talk to, perhaps. The fallen timber and the black-jack thicket had interfered with me so that I wasn't sure, any more, that I was heading straight for the fire. Down into a deep gulch I must plunge, and up I toiled, on the other side. It was about time that I climbed a tree, or did something else, to locate that fire. When next I reached a ridgy spot I chose a good pine and shinned it. From the top nothing was visible except the same old sea of timber with island rocks spotting it here and there, and with Pilot Peak and the snowy range in the wrong quarter again.

Of course, by this time the breakfast smoke would have quit. That made me desperate. I shinned down so fast that a branch broke and I partly fell the rest of the way along the trunk, and tore my shirt and scraped a big patch of skin from my chest. This hurt. When I landed in a heap I wanted to bawl. But instead, I struck off along the ridge, keeping high so that if there was smoke I would see it, yet.

The ridge ended in another gulch. I had begun to hate gulches. A fellow's legs grow numb when he hasn't had much to eat. But into the gulch I must go, and so down I plunged again. And when almost at the bottom I smelled smoke! I stopped short, and sniffed. It was wood smoke — camp smoke. I must be near that camp-fire. And away off I could hear water running. That was toward my left, so probably the smoke was on my left, for a camp would be near water. It is hard to get direction just by smell, but I turned and scouted along the side of the gulch, halfway up, sniffing and looking.

The brush was bad. It was as thick as hay and full of stickers, but I worked my way through. If the camp was the camp of the beaver man with the message, I must reconnoiter and scheme; if it was the camp of somebody else, I would go down; and if I didn't know whose camp it was, I must wait and find out.

The brush held me and tripped me and tore my trousers and shirt, and was wet and hot at the same time. Keeping high, I worked along listening and sniffing and spying—feeling for that camp, if it was a camp. Pretty soon I heard voices. That was encouraging—unless the beaver man had company. The brush thinned, and the gulch opened, and I was at the mouth of it, with the water sounding louder. On my stomach I looked out and down— and there was the place of the camp, at the mouth of the gulch, where the pines and spruces met a creek, and two boys were just leaving it. They had packs on their backs, and they were dressed in khaki and were neat and trim.

Down I went, sliding and leaping, head first or feet first, I didn't care which, as long as I got there in time. The boys heard and turned and stared,wondering. With my hands and face scratched, and my chest skinned and my shirt and trousers torn, bearing my bow and my broken arrow, like a wild boy I burst out upon them. Then suddenly I saw on the sleeves of their khaki shirts the Scout badge. My throat was too dry and my breath was too short for me to say a word, but I stopped and made the Scout sign. They answered it; and they must have thought that I was worse than I really was, because they came running.

"The Elk Patrol, Colorado," I wheezed.

"The Red Fox Patrol, New Jersey," they replied. "What's the matter?"

"I'm glad to meet you," I said, silly after the run I had made on an empty stomach; and we laughed and shook hands hard.

They were bound to hold me up or examine me for wounds or help me in some way, but I sat down of my own accord, to get my breath.

They were First-class Scouts of the Red Fox Patrol of New Jersey, and were traveling through this way on foot, from Denver, to meet the rest of their party further on at the railroad, to do Salt Lake and then the Yellowstone.

They had had a late breakfast and a good clean-up, because this was Sunday; and now they were starting on, for a walk while it was cool, before they lay by again and waited till Monday morning. I had reached them just in time; I think I'd have had tough work trailing them. They looked as if they could travel some.

Their clothes were the regulation Scouts uniform. One of them had a splendid little twenty-two rifle, and the other had a camera. The name of the boy with the rifle was Edward Van Sant; the name of the Scout with the camera was Horace Ward. They seemed fine fellows—as Scouts usually are.

I don't know how they knew that I was hungry or faint, for I didn't say that I was. But the first thing I did know Van Sant had unstrapped his pack, and Ward had taken a little pan and had brought water from the creek. Then a little alcohol stove appeared, and while we talked the water was boiling, in a jiffy. Ward dropped into the water a cube, and stirred—and there was a mess of soup, all ready!

They made me drink it, although I kept telling them I was all right. It tasted mighty good. They got out some first-aid dope, and washed my skinned chest with a carbolic smelling wash and shook some surgical powder over it, and put a bandage around, in great shape. Then they washed my scratches and even sewed the worst of the tears in my clothes.

By this time they knew my story.

"Was he a dark-complexioned man, with a small face and no whiskers or mustache?"

"He was dark, but he had a mustache and fresh whiskers," I answered.

"On a bay horse?"

"On a bay, with a blazed forehead. Why?"

"A man rode by here, last evening, along the trail across the creek. He was dark-complexioned, he wore a black hat, and he rode a bay with a mark on its shoulders like this—" and Ward drew in the dirt a K+.

"That's a K Cross," I exclaimed. And I thought it was right smart of them to notice even the brand. "He's the man, sure. He's shaved off his mustache and whiskers, but he's riding the same horse." And I jumped up. I felt strong and ready again. "Which way did he go?"

Scout Van Sant pointed up the creek. "There's a trail on the other side," he said. "You'll find fresh hoof marks in it."

"Bueno," I said; and I extended my hand to shake with them, for I must light right out. "I'm much obliged for everything, but I've got to catch him. If you meet any of my crowd please tell 'em you saw me and I'm O. K.; and if you're ever in Elk country don't fail to look us up. The lodge door is always open."

"Hold on," laughed Scout Ward. "You can't shoo us this way, unless you'd rather travel alone. What's the matter with our going, too?"

"Sure," said Scout Van Sant.

"But your trail lies down creek, you said."

"Not now. As long as you're in trouble your trail is our trail."

Wasn't that fine! But—

"You'll miss your connections with the rest of your party," I objected.

"What if we do? We're on the Scout trail, now, for business,—and pleasure can wait. You couldn't handle that man alone—could you?"

Well, I was going to try. But they wouldn't listen. And they wouldn't let me carry anything. They slung their packs on their backs, we crossed the creek on some stones, and taking the trail on the other side we followed fast and steady, the horse's hoof-prints pointing up the creek. One shoe had a bent nail-head.

The Red Fox Scouts stepped along without asking any odds, although I was traveling light. They walked like Indians. Scout Van Sant took the lead, Scout Ward came next, and I closed the rear. Pretty soon Scout Van Sant dropped back, behind me, and let Ward have the lead. I surmised he did this to watch how I was getting on; but I had that soup in me, and my second wind, and I didn't ask any odds, either.

The hoof-prints were plain, and the trail was first rate; sometimes in the timber and sometimes in little open patches, but always close to the foaming creek.

After we had traveled for about two hours, or had gone seven miles, we stopped and rested fifteen minutes and had a dish of soup. The creek branched, and one part entered a narrow, high valley, lined with much timber. The other part, which was the main part, continued more in the open.

The hoofs with the bent nail-head quit, here; and as they didn't turn off to the left, into the open country, they must have crossed to take the gulch branch. An old bridge had been washed out, but the water was shallow, and Scout Van Sant was over in about three jumps. After a minute of searching he beckoned, and we skipped over, too. A small trail followed the branch up the gulch, and the hoof-prints showed in it.

Now we all smelled smoke again. It seemed to me that I had been smelling it ever since that first time, but you know how a smell sometimes sticks in the nose. Still, we all were smelling it, now, and we kept our eyes and ears open for other sign of a camp.

The water made a big noise as it dashed down; the gulch turned and twisted, and was timbered and rocky; it grew narrower; and as we advanced with Scout caution, looking ahead each time as far as we could, on rounding an angle suddenly we came out into a sunny little park, with flowers and grass and aspens and bowlders, the stream dancing through at one edge, and an old dug-out beside the stream.

It was an abandoned prospect claim, because on the hill-slope were some old prospect holes and a dump. By the looks, nobody had been working these holes for a year or two; but from the chimney of the dug-out a thin smoke was floating. We instantly sat down, motionless, to reconnoiter.

CHAPTER XI

THE MAN AT THE DUG-OUT

We couldn't see any sign, except those hoof-marks, and that fire. Nobody was stirring, the sun shone and the chipmunks scampered and the aspens quivered and the stream tinkled, and the place seemed all uninhabited by anything except nature. We grew tired of waiting.

"I'll go on to that dug-out," whispered Scout Ward. "If the man sees me he won't know me, especially. I can find out if he's there, or who is there."

That sounded good; so he dumped his pack and while Scout Van Sant and I stayed back he walked out, up the trail. We saw him turn in at the dug-out and rap on the door. Nobody came. He hung about and eyed the trail and the ground, and rapped again.

"There's plenty of sign," he called to us; "and there's a loose horse over across the creek."

"Well, what of it?" growled a voice; and he looked, and we looked, and we saw a man sitting beside a bowlder on the little slope behind the dug-out.

The man must have been watching, half hid, without moving. It was the beaver man. He had an automatic pistol in his hand. This was my business, now. So, just saying, "There he is!" I stood up and went right forward. But Scout Van Sant followed.

"I want that message," I said, as soon as I could.

"What message?" he growled back, from over his gun.

"That Scouts' message you took from the fellow who took it from us."

"Oh, hello!" he grinned. "Were you there? They let you go, did they?"

"No; I got away to follow you. I want that message."

"Why, sure," he said. "If that's all you want." And he seemed relieved. "Come and get it." He stuck his free hand behind him and fumbled, and then he held up the package.

I started right up, but Scout Ward sprang ahead of me. "I'll get it. You and Van stay behind," he bade.

He didn't wait for us to say yes, but walked for the rock; and just as he reached it, and was stretching to take the package, the man, with a big oath, jumped for him.

Jumped for him, and grabbed for him, sprawling out like a black cougar. Van Sant and I yelled, sharp; Ward dodged and tripped and went rolling;and as the man jumped for him again I shot my arrow at him. I couldn't help it, I was so mad. The arrow was crooked, where it had been mended (I really didn't try to hurt him), and maybe it went crooked; but anyway it hit him in the calf of the leg and stayed there. I didn't think I had shot so hard.

The man uttered a quick word, and sat down. His face was screwed and he glared about at us, with his pistol muzzle wavering and sweeping like a snake's tongue. That arrow probably hurt. It hadn't gone in very far, but it was stuck.

"I'll kill one of you for that," he snarled.

"No, you won't," answered Scout Ward, scrambling up and facing him. "If you killed one you'd have to kill all three, and then you'd be hanged anyway."

"You got just what was coming to you for acting so mean," added Scout Van Sant. "You grabbed for Ward and we had to protect him."

They weren't afraid, a particle, either of them; but I was the one who had shot the arrow, and all I could say was: "It isn't barbed. You can pull it out."

"Yes, and I'll get blood poisonin', mebbe," snarled the man. He kept us covered with his revolver muzzle. "You git!" he ordered.

With his other hand he worked at the arrow and pulled it out easily. The point was red, but not very far up.

"You'd better cut your trousers open, over that wound," called Scout Van Sant. "Did you have on colored underdrawers?"

"None o' your business," snarled the man. "You git, all of you."

"Wait a minute. Don't use that old handkerchief," spoke Scout Ward. And away he ran for the packs. They were very busy Scouts, those two, and right up to snuff. The arrow wound seemed to interest them. He came back, and I saw what he had. "Here," he called; "if you'll promise not to grab me I'll come and dress that in first-class shape. You're liable to have an infection, from dirt."

"I'll infect you, if I ketch you," snarled the man, fingering his wounded leg and dividing his glances between it and us.

"Well, if you won't promise, I'll lay this on this rock," continued Scout Ward, as cool as you please. "You ought to cut the cloth away from that wound; then you dissolve this bichloride of mercury tablet in a quart of water, and flush that hole out thoroughly; then you moisten a pad of this cloth in the water and bind it on the hole with this surgical bandage. See?"

"I'll bind you on a hole, if I ketch you," snarled the man. That hole ached, I reckon.

But Scout Ward advanced and laid the first-aid stuff on a stone about ten feet from the man, so that he could crawl and get it.

"Now hadn't you better give us that message? It's no good to you, and it's done you harm enough," said Scout Van Sant.

"Give you nothin', except a dose of lead, if you don't git out pronto," snarled the man. "You git! Hear me? GIT! If you weren't kids, you'd git something else beside jes' git. But I'm not goin' to tell you many more times. GIT!"

The Red Fox Patrol Scouts looked at me and I looked at them, and we agreed—for the man was growing angrier and angrier. There was no sense in badgering him. A fellow must use discretion, you know.

"All right; we'll 'git,'" answered Scout Ward. "But we'll keep on your trail till you turn over that message. You've no business with it."

The man just growled, and as we turned away he began to pull his trouser-leg up further and to fuss with his dirty sock and his pink underdrawers there. Those were no things to have about an open wound.

"You'd better use that first-aid wash and bandage," called back Scout Ward.

We went to the packs and the Red Fox Patrol Scouts slung them on. They wouldn't let me carry one. We didn't know exactly what to do, now:whether to go on and wait, or wait here, while we watched. Only —

"You Scouts take the trail for your rendezvous," I said. Rendezvous, you know, is the place where Scouts come together; and these two boys were on their way to meet the rest of their party, for Salt Lake and the Yellowstone, when I had come in on them.

"No," they said; "your trail is our trail. Scouts help each other. We can meet our party somewhere later, and still be in time."

Scouts mean what they say, so I didn't argue, and I was mighty glad to have them along. We decided to follow the trail we were on for a little way, and then to climb the side of the gulch and make Sunday camp where we could watch the man's movements.

We passed the dug-out; up back of it the beaver man was tying his bandanna handkerchief around his leg! He didn't look at us, and he hadn't touched the first-aid stuff on the rock.

As we hiked on, I kept noticing that smell of smoke—a piny smoke; and it did not come from the dug-out, surely. Now I remembered that I had been smelling that piny smoke all day, and I laid it to the two camp-fires, but I must have been mistaken. Or else there was another fire, still—or I had the smell in my nose and couldn't get it out. When you are in the habit of smelling for something, you keep thinking that it is there, all the time. A Scout must watch his imagination, and not be fooled by it.

We climbed the side of the gulch, through the trees; the Red Fox boys carried their packs right along, without resting any more than I did. They were toughened to the long trail. The sun began to be clouded and hazy. When we halted halfway up, and looked back and down, at the dug-out, the man had hobbled across from the dug-out and was leading back his horse.

Just then Scout Ward spoke up. "It is smoke!" he exclaimed, puffing and sniffing. "Boys, it's a forest fire somewhere."

So they had been smelling it, too.

I looked at the sun. The haze clouding it was the smoke!

"Climb on top, so we can see," I said; and away we went.

The timber was thick with spruces and pines. Up we went, among them, for the top of the ridge. We came out into an open space; beyond, the ridge fell away in a long slope of the timber, for the snowy range; and old Pilot Peak was right before us, to the west. The sun was getting low, and was veiled by smoke drifting across it. And on the right, distant a couple of miles, up welled a great brownish-black mass from the fire itself.

A forest fire, and a big one! The smell was very strong.

The Red Fox Scouts looked at me. "What ought we to do?" asked Scout Van Sant. "Maybe you know more about these forest fires than we do."

Maybe I did. The Rockies are places for big forest fires, all right, and I'd heard the Guards and Rangers talk, in our town. The timber was dry as a bone, at this time of year. The smoke certainly was drifting our way. And fire travels up-hill faster than it travels down-hill. So this ridge, surrounded by the timber, was a bad spot to be caught in, especially if that fire should split and come along both sides. No timber ridge for us!

"Turn back and make for the creek; shall we?" proposed Scout Ward.

That didn't sound good to me, somehow. The creek was beginning to pinch out, this high up the gulch, and a fire would jump it in a twinkling. And if anything should happen to us, down there,—one of us hurt himself, you know, in hurrying,—we should be in a trap as the fire swept across. Out of the timber was the place for us.

But away across, an opposite slope rose to bareness, where were just grass and rocks; and between was a long patch of aspens or willows, down in the hollow. If we couldn't make the bareness, those aspens or willows would be better than the pines and evergreens. They wouldn't burn so; and if they were willows, they might be growing in a bog.

"No," I said. "Let's strike across," and I explained.

"But the man. Wait a minute. Maybe he doesn't know," said Scout Van Sant; and away he raced, down and back for the dug-out.

We followed, for of course we wouldn't let him go alone. As we ran we all shouted, and at the dug-out we shouted, looking; but all that we saw was the beaver man far off across the creek, riding through the timber. He did not glance back; he kept on, riding slowly, headed for the fire. That seemed bad. He was so angry that perhaps his judgment wasn't working right, and he didn't pay much attention to the smell of smoke. So all we could do was to race up the ridge again, get the packs, and plunge down over for sanctuary.

The wind was blowing toward the fire, as if sucked in. But I knew that this would not hold the fire, because there would be another breeze, low, carrying it along. With a big fire there always is a wind, sucked in from all sides, as the hot air rises.

Those Red Fox Scouts hiked well, loaded with their packs. I set the pace, in a bee-line for the willows and aspens, and I was traveling light, but they hung close behind. The altitude made them puff; they fairly wheezed as we zigzagged down, among the trees; but we must get out of this brush into the open.

"Will we make it?" puffed Ward.

"Sure," I said. But I was mighty anxious. It seemed to me that the distance lengthened and lengthened and that I could feel the air getting warm in puffs. This was imagination.

"Look!" cried Van Sant. "What's that?" He stopped and panted and pointed.

"Bunch of deer!" cried Ward.

It was. Not a bunch, exactly, but two does and three fawns, scampering through the timber below, fleeing from the fire. They were bounding over brush and over logs, their tails lifted showing the white—and next they were out of sight in a hollow. They made a pretty sight, but—

"Frightened by the fire, aren't they?" asked Scout Van Sant, quietly, as we jogged on.

"Yes," I had to say.

This looked serious. The fire might not be coming, and again it might. Animals are wise.

The smoke certainly was worse. The air certainly was warmer. The breeze was changing, or else we were down into another breeze. Next I saw a black, shaggy creature lumbering past, before, and I pointed without stopping. They nodded.

"Bear?" panted Ward.

I nodded. The bear was getting out of the way, too.

"Will we make it?" again asked Ward.

"Sure," I answered. We had to.

On we plowed. We were almost at the bottom of the slope and we ought to be reaching those willows and aspens. The brush was not so bad, now; but the brush does not figure much in a forest fire when the flames leap from tree-top to tree-top and make a crown fire. That is the worst of all. This was hot enough to be a crown fire, if a breeze helped it.

We saw lots of animals—rabbits and squirrels and porcupines and more deer, and the birds were calling and fluttering. The smoke rasped our throats; the air was thick with it and with the smell of burning pine. And how we sweat.

Then, hurrah! We were into the aspens. I tell you, their white trunks and their green leaves looked good to me; but ahead of us was that other slope to climb, before we were into the bareness.

"Shall we go on?" asked Scout Van Sant.

He coughed; we all coughed, as we wheezed. That had been a hard hike. The air was hot, we could feel the fire as the wind came in strong puffs; everywhere animals were running and flying, and the aspens were full of wild things, panicky. We had to decide quickly, for the fire was much closer.

"Are you good for another pull?" I asked.

They grinned, out of streaming faces and white lips.

"We'll make it if you can."

But I didn't believe that we could. Up I went into an aspen, to reconnoiter.

"Be looking for wetness, or willows," I called down. They dropped their packs and scurried.

CHAPTER XII

FOILING THE FIRE

I don't know what a record I made in climbing that tree—an aspen's bark is slick—but in a jiffy I was at the top and could peer out. All the sky was smoke, veiling the upper end of the valley and of the ridge. The ridge must be afire; the fire was spreading along our side; and if we tried for the opposite slope and the bare spot we might be caught halfway! Something whisked through the trees under me. It was a coyote. And as I slid down like lightning, thinking hard as to what we must do and do at once, I heard a calling and Van Sant and Ward came rushing back.

"We've found a place!" they cried huskily. "A boggy place, with willows. Let's get in it."

We grabbed the packs. I carried one, at last. Scout Ward led straight for the place. Willows began to appear, clustering thick. That was a good sign. The ground grew wet and soft, and slushed about our feet. I tell you, it felt fine!

"Will it do?" gasped Scout Ward, back.

"Great!" I said.

"It's occupied, but I guess we can squeeze in," added Van Sant.

And sure enough. Animals had got here first; all kinds—coyotes, rabbits, squirrels, skunks, porcupines, a big gray wolf, and a brown bear, and one or two things whose names I didn't know. But we didn't care. We forced right in, to the very middle; nothing paid much attention to us, except to step aside and give us room. Of course the coyotes snarled and so did the wolf; but the bear simply lay panting, he was so fat. And we lay panting, too.

We weren't any too soon. The air was gusty hot and gusty coolish, and the smoke came driving down. We dug holes, so that the water would collect, and so that we could dash it over each other if necessary. I could reach with my hand and pet a rabbit, but I didn't. Nothing bothered anything else.

Even the coyotes and the wolf let the rabbits alone. This was a sanctuary. There was a tremendous crashing, and a big doe elk bolted into the midst of us. She was thin and quivery, and her tongue was hanging out and her eyes staring. But she didn't stay; with another great bound she was off, outrunning the fire. She probably knew where she was going.

We others lay around, flat, waiting.

"Wish we were on her back," gasped Van Sant.

"We're all right," I said.

"Think so?"

"Sure," I answered.

They were game, those Red Fox Scouts. They never whimpered. We had done the best we could, and after you've done the best you can there is nothing left except to take what comes. And take it without kicking. As for me, I was full of thought. I never had been in a forest fire, before, but it seemed to me our chances were good. Only, I wondered about General Ashley and Fitzpatrick, in the hands of that careless gang; and about Major Henry and Jed Smith and Kit Carson, and about the beaver man with the wounded leg. He'd have the hardest time of all.

Now the smoke was so heavy and sharp that we coughed and choked. The air was scorching. We could hear a great crackling and snapping and the breeze withered the leaves about us. We burrowed. The animals around us cringed and burrowed. The fire was upon us—and a forest fire in the evergreen country is terrible.

There was a constant dull roar; our willows swayed and writhed; the rabbit crept right against me and lay shivering, and the coyotes whimpered. I flattened myself, and so did the Red Fox Scouts; and with my face in the ooze I tried to find cool air.

The roaring was steady; and the crackling and snapping was worse than any Fourth of July. Sparks came whisking down through the willows and sizzled in the wetness. One lit on a coyote and I smelled burning hair; and then one lit on me and I had to turn over and wallow on my back to put it out. "Ouch!" exclaimed Van Sant; and one must have lit on him, too.

But that was not bad. If we could stand the heat, and not swallow it and burn our lungs, we needn't mind the sparks; and maybe in ten or fifteen minutes the worst would be over, when the branches and the brush had burned.

Of course the first few moments were the ticklish ones. We didn't know what might happen. But we never said a word. Like the animals we just waited, and hoped for the best. When I found that we weren't being burned, and that the roaring and the crackling weren't harming us, I lifted my head. I sat up; and the Red Fox Scouts sat up, cautiously. We were still all right. The air was smoky, but the fire hadn't got at us—and now it probably wouldn't. But this was not at all like Sunday!

The Red Fox Scouts were pale, under their mud; and so was I, I suppose. I felt pale, and I felt weak and shaky—and I felt thankful. That had been a mighty narrow escape for us. If we had not found the willows and the wet, we would have died, it seemed to me.

"How about it?" asked Scout Ward, huskily, and his voice trembled, but I didn't blame him for that. "It's gone past, hasn't it?"

"Yes," said I. And—

"We're still here," said Scout Van Sant.

"Well," said Ward, soberly—and smiling, too, with cracked lips, "I know how I feel, and I guess you fellows feel the same way. God was good to us, and I want to thank Him."

And we kept silent a moment, and did.

The roaring had about quit and the crackling was not nearly so bad. The air was not fiery hot, any more; it was merely warm. The attack had passed, and we were safe. The rabbit beside me hopped a few feet and squatted again, and the fat bear sat up and blinked about him with his piggish eyes. It seemed to me that the animals were growing uneasy and that perhaps the truce was over with. In that case, unpleasant things were likely to happen, so we had better move out.

"Shall we try it?" asked Van Sant.

We picked up the packs and sticking close together moved on—dodging another gray wolf and a coyote, and an animal that looked like a carcajou or wolverine, which snarled at us and wouldn't budge.

Of course, it was a little doubtful whether we could travel through burned timber so soon after the fire had swept it. The ground would be thick with coals and hot ashes, and trees would still be blazing. But when we came out at the opposite edge of the willows and could see through the aspens, the timber beyond did not look bad, after all. There were a few burned places, but the fire had skirted the aspens on this side only in spots, where cinders had lodged.

So if we had kept going instead of having stopped in the willows we might have reached the place beyond all right; but it would have been taking an awful risk, and we decided that we had done the correct thing.

Smoke still hung heavy and the smell of burning pine was strong, as we threaded our way among the hot spots, making for the ridge beyond. That bare place would be a good lookout, and we rather hankered for it, anyway. We had crossed the valley, and as we climbed the slope we could look back. The fire had covered both sides of the first ridge, and the top, and if we had stayed there we would have been goners, sure, the way matters turned out. It was a dismal sight, and ought to make anybody feel sorry. Thousands of acres of fine timber had been killed—just wasted.

"What do you suppose started it?" asked Scout Ward.

A camp-fire, probably. Lots of people, camping in the timber, either don't know anything or else are out-and-out careless, like that gang from town, or those two recruits who had not made good. And I more than half believed that the fire might have started from their camps.

All of a sudden we found that we were hungry. I had been hungry before the fire, because I hadn't had much to eat for twenty-four hours; but during the fire I had forgotten about it; and now we all were hungry. However, after that fire we were nervous, in the timber, and we knew that if we camped there we wouldn't sleep. So we pushed on through, to camp on top, in the bare region, where we would be out of danger and could see around. The Red Fox canteens would give us water enough.

We came out on the bare spot. Away off to the right, along the side of the ridge, figures were moving. They were human figures, not more wild animals: two men and a pack burro. They were moving toward us, so we obliqued toward them, with our shadows cast long by the low sun. The grass was short and the footing was hard gravel, so that we could hurry; and soon I was certain that I knew who those three figures were. One was riding.

The side of the ridge was cut by a deep gulch, like a canyon, with rocky walls and stream rolling through along the bottom. We halted on our edge, and the three figures came on and halted on their edge. They were General Ashley and Fitzpatrick the Bad Hand, and Apache the black burro. The general was riding Apache. I was glad to see them.

"They're the two Elk Scouts who were captured," I said, to the Red Fox Scouts; and I waved and grinned, and they waved back, and we all exchanged the Scout sign.

But that gorge lay between, and the water made such a noise that we couldn't exchange a word.

"Can they read Army and Navy wigwags?" asked Scout Ward.

"Sure," I said. "Can you?"

"Pretty good," he answered. "Shall I make a talk, or will you?"

But I wasn't very well practiced in wigwags, yet; I was only a Second-class Scout.

"You," I said. "Do you want a flag?"

But he said he'd use his hat.

He made the "attention" signal; and Fitzpatrick answered. Then he went ahead, while Scout Van Sant spelled it out for me:

"R–e–d F–o–x."

And Fitz answered, like lightning:

"E–l–k."

"What shall I say?" asked Scout Ward of me, over his shoulder.

"Say we're all right, and ask them how they are."

He did. Scout Van Sant spelled the answer:

"O. K. B–u–t c–a–n–t c–r–o–s–s. C–a–m–p t–i–l–l m–o–r–n–i–n–g. A–s–h h–u–r–t."

When we learned that General Ashley was hurt, and knew that he and Fitzpatrick the Bad Hand were going to camp on the other side for the night, the two Red Fox Scouts, packs and all, and I got through that gulch somehow and up and out, where they were. It would have been a shame to let a one-armed boy tend to the camp and to a wounded companion, and do everything, if we could possibly help. Of course, Fitz would have managed. He was that kind. He didn't ask for help.

They were waiting; Fitz had unpacked the burro and was making camp. General Ashley was sitting with his back against a rock. He looked pale and worn. He had sprained his ankle, back there when we had all tried to escape, yesterday, and it was swollen horribly because he had had to step on it some and hadn't been able to give it the proper treatment. Fitz looked worn, too, and of course we three others (especially I) showed travel, ourselves.

After I had introduced the Red Fox Scouts to him and Fitz, then before anything else was told I must report. So I did. But I hated to say it. I saluted, and blurted it out:

"I followed the beaver man and sighted him, sir, but he got away again, with the message."

The general did not frown, or show that he was disappointed or vexed. He tried to smile, and he said: "Did he? That surely was hard luck then, Jim. Where did he go?"

"We were with Bridger, and it seems to us that he did the best he could. The fire interrupted," put in Red Fox Scout Van Sant, hesitatingly.

He spoke as if he knew that he had not been asked for an opinion, but as a friend and as a First-class Scout he felt as though he ought to say something.

"The best is all that any Scout can do," agreed the general. "Go ahead, Jim, and tell what happened."

So I did. The general nodded. I hadn't made any excuses; I tried to tell just the plain facts, and ended with our escape in the willows, from that fire.

"The report is approved," he said. "We'll get that beaver man yet. We must have that message. Now Fitz can tell what happened to us. But we'd better be sending up smoke signals to call in the other squad, in case they're where they can see. Make the council signal, Bridger."

Fitz had a fire almost ready; the Red Fox Scouts helped me, and gathered smudge stuff while I proceeded to send up the council signal in the Elks code. Fitz talked while he worked. The general looked on and winced as his ankle throbbed. But he was busy, too, fighting pain.

Fitz told what had happened to them, after I had escaped. He and the general had been taken back by the gang, and tied again, and camp was broken in a hurry because the gang feared that now I would lead a rescue. They were mean enough to make the general limp along, without bandaging his foot, until he was so lame that he must be put on a horse. The camp-fire was left burning and the bacon was forgotten. They climbed a plateau and dropped into a flat, and following up very fast had curved into the timber to cross another ridge into Lost Park and on for the Divide by way of Glacier Lake. That is what the general and Fitz guessed. That night they all camped on the other side of the timber ridge, at the edge of Lost Park. They were in a hurry, still, and they made their fire in the midst of trees where they had no business to make it. They slept late, as they always did, and not having policed the camp or put out their fire, scarcely had they plunged into Lost Park, the next morning, when one of them looking back saw the trees afire where they had been.

Lost Park is a mean place; the brush makes a regular jungle of it, and fire would go through it as through a hayfield. That fact and their guilty conscience made them panicky. It's a pretty serious thing, to start a forest fire. So they didn't know what to do; some wanted to go one way, and some another; the fire grew bigger and bigger, and the cattle and game trails wound and twisted and divided so that the gang were separated, in the brush, and it was every man for himself. The general was riding Mike Delavan's horse, and Mike ordered him down and climbed on himself and made off; and the first thing the general and Fitz knew they were abandoned. That is what they would have maneuvered for, from the beginning, and it would have been easy, as Scouts, to work it, among those blind trails, but the general couldn't walk. Perhaps it was by a mistake that they were abandoned; everybody may have thought that somebody else was tending to them, and Mike didn't know what he was doing, he was so excited. But there they were.

The general tried to hobble, and Fitz was bound that he would carry him — good old Fitz, with the one arm! The bushes were high, the smoke where the fire was mounted more and more and spread as if the park was doomed, and the crashing and shouting and swearing of the gang faded and died away in the distance. Then the general and Fitz heard something coming, and down the trail they were on trotted Apache the burro! He must have turned back or have entered by a cross trail. Whew, but they were glad to see Apache! Fitz grabbed him by the neck rope. He had a flat pack tied on with our rope, did Apache, and Fitz hoisted the general aboard, and away they hiked, with the general hanging on and his foot dangling.

Now that they could travel and head as they pleased, they worked right back, out of the park, and by a big circuit so as not to run into the gang they circled the fire and tried to strike the back trail somewhere so as to meet Major Henry and Carson and Smith, who might be on it. But they came out upon this plateau, and sighted us, and then we all met at the edge of the gulch.

That was the report of Fitzpatrick the Bad Hand. He and the general certainly had been through a great deal.

During the story the Red Fox Scouts and I had been making the smoke signal over and over again. "Come to council," I sent up, while they helped to keep the smudge thick. "Come to council," "Come to council," for Major Henry and Kit and Jed, wherever they might be. But we were so interested in Fitz's story, how he and the general got away from the gang and from the fire, that sometimes we omitted to scan the horizon. The general didn't, though. He is a fine Scout.

"There's the answer!" he said suddenly. "They've seen! The fire didn't get them. Hurrah!"

And "Hurrah!" we cheered.

CHAPTER XIII

ORDERS FROM THE PRESIDENT

(THE ADVENTURES OF THE MAJOR HENRY PARTY)

I am Tom Scott, or Major Andrew Henry, second in command of the Elk Patrol Scouts which set out to take that message over the range. So now I will make a report upon what happened to our detail after General Ashley and Fitzpatrick and Bridger left, upon the trail of the two boys who had stolen our flags and burros.

We waited as directed all day and all night, and as they did not come back or make any signal, in the morning we prepared to follow them. First we sent up another smoke for half an hour, and watched for an answer; but nothing happened. Then we cached the camp stuff by rolling in the bedding, with the tarpaulins on the outside, what we couldn't carry, and stowing it under a red spruce. The branches came down clear to the ground, in a circle around, and when we had crawled in and had covered the bundle with other boughs and needles, it couldn't be seen unless you looked mighty close.

We erased our tracks to the tree, and made two blazes, on other trees, so that our cache was in the middle of a line from blaze to blaze. Then we took sights, and wrote them down on paper, so that none of us would forget how to find the place.

We each had a blanket, rolled and slung in army style, with a string run through and tied at the ends. I carried the twenty-two rifle, and we stuffed away in our clothes what rations we could. In my blanket I carried the other of our lariat ropes. We might need it.

So the time was about ten o'clock before we started. The trail was more than twenty-four hours old, but our Scouts had made it plain on purpose, and we followed right along. Of course, I am sixteen and Kit Carson is thirteen and little Jed Smith is only twelve, so I set my pace to theirs. A blanket roll weighs heavy after you have carried it a few miles.

But we stopped only twice before we reached a sign marked in the ground: "Look out!" The trail faltered, and an arrow showed which way to go, and we came to the spot where the Scouts had peeped over into the draw and had seen the enemy. Here another arrow pointed back, and we understood exactly what had happened.

We took the new direction. The three Scouts had left as plain a trail as they could by breaking branches and disturbing pebbles, and treading in single file. Jed Smith was awful tired, by this time, for the sun was hot and we hadn't halted to eat. But picking the trail we made the circuit around the upper end of the draw and climbed the opposite ridge. The trail was harder to read, here, among the grass and rocks.

By the sun it was the middle of the afternoon, now, and we must have been on the trail five hours. We waited, and listened, and looked and smelled, feeling for danger. We must not run into any ambuscade. A little gulch, with timber, lay just ahead, and a haze of smoke floated over it.

This spelled danger. It was not Scouts' smoke, because Scouts would not be having a fire, at this time of day, smoking so as to betray their position. When we made a smoke, we made it for a purpose. The place must be reconnoitered.

We spread. I took the right, Kit Carson the left, and Jed Smith was put in the middle because he was the littlest. It would have been good if we could have left our blanket rolls, but we did not dare to. Of course, if we were chased, we might have to drop them and let them be captured.

We crossed a cow-path, leading into the gulch. It held burro tracks, pointing down; and it seemed to me that if there was any ambuscade down there it would be along this trail. Naturally, the enemy would expect us to follow the trail. Maybe the other Scouts had followed it and had been surrounded. So we crossed the trail, and I signed to Carson and to Smith to move out across the gulch and around by the other side.

We did. Cedars and spruces were scattered about, and gooseberry bushes and other brush were screen enough; we swung down along the opposite side, and the smoke grew stronger. But still we could not hear a sound. We closed in, peering and listening—and then suddenly I wasn't afraid, or at least, I didn't care. Through the stems of the trees was an open park, at the foot of the gulch, and if there was a camp nobody was at home, for the park was afire!

"Come on!" I shouted. "Fire!" and down I rushed. So did Carson and Jed Smith.

We were just in time. The flames had spread from an old camp-fire and had eaten along across the grass and pine needles and were among the brush, getting a good start. Already a dry stump was blazing; and in fifteen minutes more a tree somewhere would have caught. And then—whew!

But we sailed into it, stamping and kicking and driving it back from the brush.

"Wet your blanket, Jed," I ordered, "while we fight."

A creek was near, luckily; Jed wet his blanket, and we each in turn wet our blankets; and swiping with the rolls we smashed the line of fire right and left, and had it out in just a few minutes.

Now a big blackened space was left, like a blot; and the burning and our trampling about had destroyed most of the sign. But we must learn what had happened. We got busy again.

We picked up the cow-path, back in the gulch, and found that the burros had followed it this far. We found where the burros had been grazing and standing, in the brush, near the burned area, and we found where horses had been standing, too! We found fish-bones, and coffee-grounds dumped from the little bag they had been boiled in, and a path had been worn to the creek. We found in the timber and brush near by other sign, but we missed the second warning sign. However, where the fire had not reached, on the edge of the park, we found several pieces of rope, cut, lying together, and in a soft spot of the turf here we found the hob-nail prints of the Elk Patrol! By ashes we found where the main camp-fire had been, and we found where a second smaller camp-fire had been, at the edge of the park, and prints of shoes worn through in the left sole—the shoes of the beaver man! We found a tin plate and fork, by the big camp-fire, and wrapped in a piece of canvas in a spruce was a hunk of bacon. By circling we found an out-going trail of horses and burros. We found the out-going trail of the beaver man—or of a single horse, anyway, but no shoe prints with it. But looking hard we found Scout sole prints in the horse and burro trail.

By this time it was growing dusk, and Jed Smith was sick because he had drunk too much water out of the creek, when he was tired and hot and hungry. So we decided to stay here for the night. From the signs we figured out what might have happened:

According to the tracks, the burro thieves had joined with this camp. Our fellows had sighted the burro thieves, back where the "Look out" sign had been made, and had circuited the draw so as to keep out of sight themselves, and had taken the trail again on the ridge. They had followed along that cow-path, and had been ambushed. The cut ropes showed that they had been tied. This camp had been here for two or three days, because of the path worn to the creek and because of the coffee grounds and the fish bones and the other sign. It was a dirty camp, too, and with its unsanitary arrangements and cigarette butts and tobacco juice was such a camp as would be made by that town gang. The sign of the cut ropes looked like the town gang, too. The camp must have broken up in a hurry, and moved out quick, by the things that were forgotten. Campers don't forget bacon, very often. The cut ropes would show haste, and we might have thought that the Scout prisoners had escaped, if we hadn't found their sole prints with the out-going trail. These prints had been stepped on by burros, showing that the burros followed behind. What the beaver man was doing here we could not tell.

So we guessed pretty near, I think.

Little Jed Smith had a splitting headache, from heat and work and water-drinking. His tongue looked all right, so I decided it was just tiredness and stomach. One of the blankets was dry; we wrapped him up and let him lie quiet, with a wet handkerchief on his eyes, and I gave him a dose of aconite, for fever.

At this time, we know now, General Ashley and Thomas Fitzpatrick were being hustled along one trail, captives to the gang; the beaver man was on a second trail, with our message; and Jim Bridger was on his lone scout in another direction, and just about to make a camp-fire with his hob-nails and a flint.

The dusk was deepening, and Kit Carson and I went ahead settling camp for the night. We built a fire, and spread the blankets, and were making tea in a tin can when we heard hoof thuds on the cow-path. A man rode in on us. He was a young man, with a short red mustache and a peaked hat, and a greenish-shade Norfolk jacket with a badge on the left breast. A Forest Ranger! Under his leg was a rifle in scabbard.

"Howdy?" he said, stopping and eying us.

Kit Carson and I saluted him, military way, because he represented the Government, and answered: "Howdy, sir?"

He was cross, as he gazed about.

"What are you lads trying to do? Set the timber afire?" he scolded. He saw the burned place, you know.

"We didn't do that," I answered. "It was afire when we came in and we put it out."

He grunted.

"How did it start?"

"A camp-fire, we think."

He fairly snorted. He was pretty well disgusted and angered, we could see.

"Of course. There are more blamed fools and down-right criminals loose in these hills this summer than ever before. I've done nothing except chase fires for a month, now. Who are you fellows?"

"We're a detail of the Elk Patrol, 14th Colorado Troop, Boy Scouts of America."

"Well, I suppose you've been taught about the danger from camp-fires, then?"

"Yes, sir," I answered.

"Bueno," he grunted. "Wish there were plenty more like you. Every person who leaves a live camp-fire behind him, anywhere, ought to be made to stay in a city all the rest of his life."

He straightened in his saddle and lifted the lines to ride on. But his horse looked mighty tired and so did he; and as a Scout it was up to me to say: "Stop off and have supper. We're traveling light, but we can set out bread and tea."

"Sure," added Kit Carson and Jed Smith.

"No, thanks," he replied. "I've got a few miles yet to ride, before I quit. And to-morrow's Sunday, when I don't ride much if I can help it. So long."

"So long," we called; and he passed on at a trot.

We had supper of bread and bacon and tea. The bread sopped in bacon grease was fine. Jed felt better and drank some tea, himself, and ate a little. It was partly a hunger headache. We pulled dead grass and cut off spruce and pine tips, and spread a blanket on it all. The two other blankets we used for covering. Our coats rolled up were pillows. We didn't undress, except to take off our shoes. Then stretched out together, on the one-blanket bed and under the two blankets, we slept first-rate. Jed had the warm middle place, because he was the littlest.

As I was commander of the detail I woke up first in the morning, and turned out. After a rub-off at the creek I took the twenty-two and went hunting for breakfast. I saw a rabbit; but just as I drew a bead on him I suddenly remembered that this was Sunday morning — and I quit. Sunday ought to be different from other days. So I left him hopping and happy, and I went back to camp. Jed and Kit had the fire going and the water boiling; and we breakfasted on tea and bread and bacon.

Then we policed the camp, put out the fire, every spark, and took the burro and horse trail, to the rescue again. We must pretend that this was only a little Sunday walk, for exercise.

After a while the trail crossed the creek at a shallow place, and by a cow-path climbed the side of a hill. Before exposing ourselves on top of the hill we crawled and stuck just our heads up, Indian scouts fashion, to reconnoiter. The top was clear of enemy. Sitting a minute, to look, we could see old Pilot Peak and the snowy range where we Scouts ought to be crossing, bearing the message. We believed that now the gang with prisoners were traveling to cross the range, too. They had the message, of course, and that was bad, unless we could head them off. So we sort of hitched our belts another notch and traveled as fast as we could.

The hill we were on spread into a plateau of low cedars and scrubby pines; the snowy range, with Pilot Peak sticking up, was before. After we had been hiking for two or three hours, off diagonally to the left we saw a forest fire. This was thick timber country, and the fire made a tremendous smoke. It was likely to be a big fire, and we wondered if the ranger was fighting it. As for us, we were on the trail and must hurry.

We watched the fire, but we were not afraid of it, yet. The plateau was too bare for it, if it came our way. The smoke grew worse — a black, rolling smoke; and we could almost see the great sheets of flame leaping. We were glad we weren't in it, and that we didn't know of anybody else who was in it. But whoever had set it had done a dreadful thing.

The trail of the burros and of the horses, mixed, continued on, and left the plateau and dipped down into a wide flat, getting nearer to the timber on the slope opposite. Then out from our left, or on the fire side, a man came riding hard. He shouted and waved at us, so we stopped.

He was the Ranger. I tell you, but he looked tired and angry. His eyes were red-rimmed and his face was streaked with sweat and dirt, and holes were burned in his clothes and his horse's hide.

"I want you boys," he panted, as soon as he drew up. "We've got to stop that fire. See it?"

Of course we'd seen it. But—it wasn't any of our business, was it?

"I want you to hurry over there to a fire line and keep the fire from crossing. Quick! Savvy?"

"I don't believe we can, sir," I said. "We're on the trail."

"What difference does that make?"

"We're after a gang who have three of our men and we want to stop them before they cross the range."

"You follow me."

"I'm sorry," I said; "but we're trailing. We're obeying orders."

"Whose orders?"

"Our Patrol leader's."

"Who's he?"

"General Ashley—I mean, Roger Franklin. He's another boy. But he's been captured and two of our partners. We're to follow and rescue them. We've got to go."

"No, you haven't," answered the Ranger. "Not until after this fire is under control. You'll be paid for your time."

"We don't care anything about the pay," said Kit Carson. "We've got to go on."

"Well, I'm giving you higher orders from a higher officer, then," retorted the Ranger. "I'm giving you orders from the President of the United States. This is Government work, and I'm representing the Government. I reckon you Boy Scouts want to support the Government, don't you?"

Sure we did.

"If that fire goes it will burn millions of dollars' worth of timber, and may destroy ranches and people, too. It's your duty now to help the Government and to put it out. Your duty to Uncle Sam is bigger than any duty to private Scouts' affairs. And it is the law that anybody seeing a forest fire near him shall report it or aid in extinguishing it. Now, are you coming, or will you sneak off with an excuse?"

"Why—coming!" we all cried at once. We hated to leave the trail—to leave the general and Fitz and Jim Bridger and the message to their fate; but the Government was calling, here, and the first duty of good Scouts is to be good citizens.

"Pass up your blanket rolls," ordered the Ranger. "You smallest kid climb behind me. Each of you two others catch hold of a stirrup. Then we can make time across."

In a second away we all went at a trot, heading for the timber and the fire.

"I rode right through that fire to get you," said the Ranger. "I saw you. I've got two or three guards working up over the ridge. Your job is to watch a fire line that runs along this side of the base of that point yonder. One end of the fire line is a boggy place with willows and aspens; and if we can keep the fire from jumping those willows and starting across, down the valley, and those fellows on the other side of the ridge can head it off, in their direction, then we'll stop it by back-firing at the edge of Brazito canyon."

He talked as rapidly as we moved—and that was good fast Scouts' trot, for us. The hold on the stirrups and latigos helped a lot. It lifted us over the ground. We all crossed the flat diagonally and struck into a draw or valley full of timber and with a creek in it, at right angles to the flat. Up this we scooted, hard as we could pelt.

"Tired? Want to rest a second?" he asked.

We grunted "No," for we had our second wind and little Jed Smith was hanging on tight, behind the saddle. Besides, the fire was right ahead, toward the left, belching up its great rolls of black-and-white smoke. And at the same time (although we didn't know it) the gang who had started it were fleeing in one direction, from it, and the general and Fitzpatrick were loose and fleeing in another direction, and Jim Bridger was smelling it and with the Red Fox Patrol was drawing near to it and not knowing, and the beaver man was tying up his leg and about to run right into it.

But we were to help stop it.

"Here!" spoke the Ranger. "Here's the fire line, this cleared space like a trail. It runs to those willows a quarter of a mile below. When the fire comes along this ridge you watch this line and beat out and stamp out every flame. See? You can do it. It won't travel fast, down-hill; but if ever it crosses the line and reaches the bottom of the valley where the brush is thick, there's no knowing where it will stop. It will burn willows and everything else. One of you drop off here; I'll take the others further. Then I must make tracks for the front."

We left Kit Carson here. Jed Smith climbed down and was left next, in the middle, and I was hustled to the upper end.

"So long," said the Ranger. "Don't let it get past you. It won't. Work hard, and if you're really in danger run for the creek. But Boy Scouts of America don't run till they have to. You can save lives and a heap of timber, by licking the fire at this point. I'll see you later." And off he spurred, through the timber, across the front of the fire.

He wasn't afraid—and so we weren't, either.

CHAPTER XIV

THE CAPTURE OF THE BEAVER MAN

The fire line looked like some old wood-road, where trees had been cut out and brush cleared away. It extended through the timber, striking the thin places and the rocky bare places, and the highest places, and wound on, half a mile, over a point. This point, with a long slope from the ridge to the valley there, was open and fire-proof. The lower end of the line was that willow bog, which lay in a basin right in a split of the timber. Away across from our ridge was another gravelly ridge, and beyond that was the snowy range.

The smoke was growing thick and strong, so that we could smell it plain. The fire was coming right along, making for us. There were the three of us to cover a half-mile or more of fire line, so we got busy. We divided the line into three patrols, and set to work tramping down the brush on the fire side of it and making ready.

Pretty soon wild animals began to pass, routed out by the fire. That was fun, to watch deer and coyotes and rabbits and other things scoot by, among the trees, as if they were moving pictures. Once I saw a wolf, and little Jed Smith called that he had seen a bear. Kit Carson reported that some of the animals seemed to be heading into the willow bog beyond his end of the line.

It was kind of nervous work, getting ready and waiting for the fire. It was worse than actual fighting, and we'd rather meet the fire halfway than wait for it to come to us. But we were here to wait.

The fire did not arrive all at once, with a jump. Not where I was. A thin blue smoke, lazy and harmless, drifted through among the trees, and a crackling sounded louder and louder. Then there were breaths of hot air, as if a dragon was foraging about. Birds flew over, calling and excited, and squirrels raced along, and porcupines and skunks, and even worms and ants crawled and ran, trying to escape the dragon. A wind blew, and the timber moaned as if hurt and frightened. I felt sorry for the pines and spruces and cedars. They could not run away, and they were doomed to be burnt alive.

The birds all had gone, worms and ants and bugs were still hurrying, and the timber was quiet except for the crackling. Now I glimpsed the dragon himself. He was digging around, up the slope a little way, extending his claws further and further like a cat as he explored new ground and gathered in every morsel.

This is the way the fire came—not roaring and leaping, but sneaking along the ground and among the bushes, with little advance squads like dragon's claws or like the scouts of an army, reconnoitering. The crackling increased, the hot gusts blew oftener, I could see back into the dragon's great mouth where bushes and trees were flaming and disappearing—and suddenly he gave a roar and leaped for our fire line, and ate a bush near it.

Then I leaped for him and struck a paw down with my stick. So we began to fight.

It wasn't a crown fire, where the flames travel through the tops of the timber; it traveled along the ground, and climbed the low trees and then reached for the big ones. But when it came near the fire line, it stopped and felt about sort of blindly, and that was our chance to jump on it and stamp it out and beat it out and kill it.

The smoke was awful, and so was the heat, but the wind helped me and carried most of it past. And now the old dragon was right in front of me, raging and snapping. The fore part of him must be approaching Jed Smith, further along the line. I whistled the Scout whistle, loud, and gave the Scout halloo—and from Jed echoed back the signal to show that all was well.

This was hot work, for Sunday or any day. The smoke choked and blinded, and the air fairly scorched. Pine makes a bad blaze. What I had to do was to run back and forth along the fire line, crushing the dragon's claws. My shoes felt burned through and my face felt blistered, and jiminy, how I sweat! But that dragon never got across my part of the fire line.

The space inside my part was burnt out and smoldering, and I could join with Jed. There were two of us to lick the fire, here; but the dragon was raging worse and the two of us were needed. He kept us busy. I suppose that there was more brush. And when we would follow him down, and help Kit, he was worse than ever. How he roared!

He was determined to get across and go around that willow bog. Once he did get across, and we chased him and fought him back with feet and hands and even rolled on him. A bad wind had sprung up, and we didn't know but that we were to have a crown fire. The heat would have baked bread; the cinders were flying and we must watch those, to catch them when they landed. We had to be everywhere at once—in the smoke and the cinders and the flames, and if I hadn't been a Scout, stationed with orders, I for one would have been willing to sit and rest, just for a minute, and let the blamed fire go. But I didn't, and Kit and Jed didn't; all of a sudden the dragon quit, and with roar and crackle went plunging on, along the ridge inside the willow bog. We had held the fire line—and we didn't know that Jim Bridger and the Red Fox Scouts were in those willows which we had saved because we had been ordered to!

Then, when just a few little blazes remained to be trampled and beaten out, but while the timber further in was still aflame, Jed cried: "Look!" and we saw a man coming, staggering and coughing, down through a rocky little canyon which cut the black, smoking slope.

He fell, and we rushed to get him.

Blazing branches were falling, all about; the air was two hundred in the shade; and in that little canyon the rocks seemed red-hot. But the fire hadn't got into the canyon, much, because it was narrow and bare; and the man must have been following it and have made it save his life. He was in bad shape, though. Before we reached him he had stood up and tumbled several times, trying to feel his way along.

"Wait! We're coming," I called. He heard, and tried to see.

"All right," he answered hoarsely. "Come ahead."

We reached him. Kit Carson and I held him up by putting his arms over our shoulders, and with Jed walking behind we helped him through the canyon and out to the fire line. He groaned and grunted. His eyebrows were crisped and his hair was singed and his shoes were cinders and his hands and face were scarred, and his eyes were all bloodshot, and he had holes through his clothes.

"Fire out?" he asked. "I can't see."

"It isn't out, but it's past," said Jed.

"Well, it mighty near got me," he groaned. "It corralled me on that ridge. If I hadn't cached myself in that little canyon, I'd have been burned to a crisp. It burned my hoss, I reckon. He jerked loose from me and left me to go it alone with my wounded leg. Water! Ain't there a creek ahead? Gimme some water."

While he was mumbling we set him down, beyond the fire line. It didn't seem as though we could get him any further. Kit hustled for water, Jed skipped to get first-aid stuff from a blanket-roll, and I made an examination.

His face and hands were blistered—maybe his eyes were scorched—there was a bloody place wrapped about with a dirty red handkerchief, on the calf of his left leg. But I couldn't do much until I had scissors or a sharp knife, and water.

"Who are you kids?" he asked. "Fishin'?" He was lying with his eyes closed.

"No. We're some Boy Scouts."

He didn't seem to like this. "Great Scott!" he complained. "Ain't there nobody but Boy Scouts in these mountains?"

Just then Kit came back with a hat of water from a boggy place. It was muddy water, but it looked wet and good, and the man gulped it down, except what I used to soak our handkerchiefs in. Kit went for more. Jed arrived with first-aid stuff, and I set to work, Jed helping.

We let the man wipe his own face, while we cut open his shirt where it had stuck to the flesh.

"Here!" he said suddenly. "Quit that. What's the matter with you?"

But he was too late. When I got inside his undershirt, there on a buckskin cord was hanging something that we had seen before. At least, it either was the message of the Elk Patrol or else a package exactly like it.

"Is that yours?" I asked.

"Maybe yes, and maybe no. Why?" he growled.

"Because if it isn't, we'd like to know where you got it."

"And if you don't tell, we'll go on and let you be," snapped little Jed.

"Shut up," I ordered—which wasn't the right way, but I said it before I thought. Jed had made me angry. "No, we won't." And we wouldn't. Our duty was to fix him the best we could. "But that looks like something belonging to us Scouts, and it has our private mark on it. We'd like to have you explain where you got it."

"He's got to explain, too," said little Jed, excited.

"Have I?" grinned the man, hurting his face. "Why so?"

"There are three of us kids. We can keep sight of you till that Ranger comes back. He'll make you."

"Who?"

"That Forest Ranger. He's a Government officer."

Kit Carson arrived, staring, with more water.

"I know you!" he panted. He signed to us, pointing at the man's feet. "You were at that other camp!" And Jed and I looked and saw the hole in the left sole—although both soles were badly burned, now. By that mark he was the beaver man! He wriggled uneasily as if he had a notion to sit up.

"Well, if you want it so bad, and it's yours, take it." And in a jiffy I had cut it loose with my knife. "It's been a hoodoo to me. How did you know I was at any other camp? Are you those three kids?"

"We saw your tracks," I answered. "What three kids?"

"The three kids those other fellows had corralled."

"No, but we're their partners. We're looking for them."

He'd had another drink of water and his face squinted at us, as we fussed about him. Kit took off one of the shoes and I the other, to get at the blistered feet.

"Never saw you before, did I?"

"Maybe not."

"Well, I'll tell you some news. One of your partners got away."

That was good.

"How do you know?" we all three asked.

"I met him, back on the trail, with two new kids."

"Which one was he? What did he look like?"

"A young lad, dressed like you. Carried a bow and arrow."

"Brown eyes and big ears?"

"Brown eyes, I reckon. Didn't notice his ears."

That must have been Jim Bridger.

"Who were the two fellows?"

"More of you Scouts, I reckon. Carried packs on their backs. Dressed in khaki and leggins, like soldiers."

They weren't any of us Elks, then. But we were tremendously excited.

"When?"

"This noon."

That sure was news. Hurrah for Jim Bridger!

"Did you see a one-armed boy?"

"Saw him in that camp, where the three of 'em were corralled."

"What kind of a crowd had they? Was one wearing a big revolver?"

"Yes. 'Bout as big as he was. They looked like some tough town bunch."

"How many?"

"Eight or ten."

Oho!

"Did you hear anybody called Bill?"

"Yes; also Bat and Mike and Walt and et cetery."

We'd fired these questions at him as fast as we could get them in edgewise, and now we knew a heap. The signs had told us true. Those two recruits had joined with the town gang, and our Scouts had been captured; but escape had been attempted and Jim Bridger had got away.

"How did you get that packet?" asked Kit.

"Found it."

He spoke short as if he was done talking. It seemed that he had told us the truth, so far; but if we kept questioning him much more he might get tired or cross, and lie. We might ask foolish questions, too; and foolish questions are worse than no questions.

We had done a good job on this man, as appeared to us. We had bathed his face, and had exposed the worst burns on his body and arms and legs and had covered them with carbolized vaseline and gauze held on with adhesive plaster, and had cleaned the wound in his leg. It was a regular hole, but we didn't ask him how he got it. 'Twas in mighty bad shape, for it hadn't been attended to right and was dirty and swollen. Cold clear water dripped into it to flush it and clean it and reduce the inflammation would have been fine, but we didn't have that kind of water handy; so we sifted some boric powder into it and over it and bound on it a pad of dry sterilized gauze, but not too tight. I asked him if there was a bullet or anything else in it, and he said no. He had run against a stick. This was about all that we could do to it, and play safe by not poking into it too much.

He seemed to feel pretty good, now, and sat up.

"Well," he said, "now I've given you boys your message and told you what I know, and you've fixed me up, so I'll be movin' on. Where are those things I used to call shoes?"

We exchanged glances. He was the beaver man.

"We aren't through yet," I said.

"Oh, I reckon you are," he answered. "I'm much obliged. Pass me the shoes, will you?"

"No; wait," said Kit Carson.

"What for?" He was beginning to growl.

"Till you're all fixed."

"I'm fixed enough."

"We'll dress some of those wounds over again."

"No, you won't. Pass me those shoes."

They were hidden behind a tree.

"Can't you wait a little?"

"No, I can't wait a little." He was growling in earnest. "Will you pass me those shoes?"

"No, we won't," announced Kit. He was getting angry, too.

"You pass me those shoes or something is liable to happen to you mighty sudden. I'll break you in two."

"I'll get the rifle," said Jed, and started; but I called him back. We didn't need a rifle.

"He can't do anything in bare feet like that," I said. And he couldn't. His feet were too soft and burned. That is why we kept the shoes, of course.

"I can't, eh?"

"No. We aren't afraid."

He started to stand, and then he sat back again.

"I'll put a hole in some of you," he muttered; and felt at the side of his chest. But if he had carried a gun in a Texas holster there, it was gone. "Say, you, what's the matter with you?" he queried. "What do you want to keep me here for?"

"You'd better wait. We'll stay, too."

He glared at us. Then he began to wheedle.

"Say, what'd I ever do to you? Didn't I give you back that message, and tell you all I knew? Didn't I help you out as much as I could?"

"Sure," we said.

"Then what have you got it in for me for?"

"We'd rather you'd wait till the Ranger or somebody comes along," I explained.

He fumbled in a pants pocket.

"Lookee here," he offered. And he held it out. "Here's a twenty-dollar gold piece. Take it and divvy it among you; and I'll go along and nobody'll be the wiser."

"No, thanks," we said.

"I'll make it twenty apiece for each," he insisted. "Here they are. See? Give me those shoes, and take these yellow bucks and go and have a good time."

But we shook our heads, and had to laugh. He couldn't bluff us Scouts, and he couldn't bribe us, either. He twisted and stood up, and we jumped away, and Kit was ready to grab up the shoes and carry them across into the burned timber where the ground was still hot.

The man swore and threatened frightfully.

"I'd like to get my fingers on one of you, once," he stormed. "You'd sing a different tune."

So we would. But we had the advantage now and we didn't propose to lose it. He couldn't travel far in bare, blistered feet. I wished that he'd sit down again. We didn't want to torment him or nag him, just because we had him. He did sit down.

"What do you think I am, anyhow?" he asked.

"Well, you've been killing beaver," I told him.

"Who said so?"

"We saw you at the beaver-pond, when we were camping opposite. And just after you left the game warden came along, looking for you."

"You saw some other man."

"No, we didn't. We know your tracks. And if you aren't the man, then you'll be let go."

"You kids make me tired," he grumbled, and tried to laugh it off. "Supposin' a man does trap a beaver or two. They're made to be trapped. They have to be trapped or else they dam up streams and overflow good land. Nobody misses a few beaver, anyhow, in the timber. This is a free land, ain't it?"

"Killing beaver is against the law, just the same," said Jed.

"You kids didn't make the law, did you? You aren't judge of the law, are you?"

"No," I said. "But we know what it is and we don't think it ought to be broken. If people go ahead breaking the game laws, then there won't be any game left for the people who keep the laws to see or hunt. And the less game there is, the more laws there'll be." I knew that by heart. It was what Scouts are taught.

This sounded like preaching. But it was true. And while he was fuming and growling and figuring on what to do, we were mighty glad to hear a horse's hoofs. The Ranger came galloping down the fire line.

"Hello," he said. He was streaked with ashes and soot and sweat, and so was his horse, and they both looked worn to a frazzle. "Well, we've licked the fire. Who's that? Somebody hurt?" Then he gave another quick look. "Why, how are you, Jack? You must have run against something unexpected."

The beaver man only growled, as if mad and disgusted.

I saluted.

"We have held the fire line, sir," I reported.

"You bet!" answered the Ranger. "You did well. And now you're holding Jack, are you? You needn't explain. I know all about him. Since that fire drove him out along with other animals, we'll hang on to him. The game warden spoke to me about him a long time ago."

"You fellows think you're mighty smart. Do I get my shoes, or not?" growled the beaver man.

"Not," answered the Ranger, cheerfully. "We'll wrap your feet up with a few handkerchiefs and let you ride this horse." He got down. "What's the matter? Burns? Bad leg? Say! These kids are some class on first-aid, aren't they! You're lucky. Did you thank them? Now you can ride nicely and the game warden will sure be glad to see you." Then he spoke to us. "I'm going over to my cabin, boys, where there's a telephone. Better come along and spend the night."

We hustled for our blanket-rolls. The beaver man gruntingly climbed aboard the Ranger's horse, and we all set out. The Ranger led the horse, and carried his rifle.

"Is the fire out?" asked Kit Carson.

"Not out, but it's under control. It'll burn itself out, where it's confined. I've left a squad to guard it and I'll telephone in to headquarters and report. But if it had got across this fire line and around those willows, we'd have been fighting it for a week."

"How did it start?"

"Somebody's camp-fire."

The trail we were making led through the timber and on, across a little creek and up the opposite slope. The sun was just setting as we came out beyond the timber, and made diagonally up a bare ridge. On top it looked like one end of that plateau we had crossed when we were trailing the gang and we had first seen the fire.

The Ranger had come up here because traveling was better and he could take a good look around. We halted, puffing, while he looked. Off to the west was the snowy range, and old Pilot Peak again, with the sun setting right beside him, in a crack. The range didn't seem far, but it seemed cold and bleak—and over it we were bound. Only, although now we had the message, we didn't have the other Scouts. If they were burned—oh, jiminy!

"Great Cæsar! More smoke!" groaned the Ranger. "If that's another fire started—!"

His words made us jump and gaze about. Yes, there was smoke, plenty of it, over where the forest fire we had fought was still alive. But he was looking in another direction, down along the top of the plateau.

"See it?" he asked.

Yes, we saw it. But—! And then our hearts gave a great leap.

"That's not a forest fire!" we cried. "That's a smoke signal!"

"A what?"

"A smoke signal! And—"

"Wait a second. We'll read it, if we can. Scouts must be over there," I exclaimed.

"More Scouts!" grunted the beaver man. "These here hills are plumb full of 'em."

The air was quiet, and the smoke rose straight up, with the sun tinting the top. It was a pretty sight, to us. Then we saw two puffs and a pause, and two puffs and a pause, and two puffs and a pause. It was our private Elk Patrol code, and it was beautiful. We cheered.

"It's from our partners, and it says 'Come to council,'" I reported. "They're hunting for us. We'll have to go over there."

"Think they're in trouble?"

"They don't say so, but we ought to signal back and go right over."

"I'll go, too, for luck, and see you through, then," said the Ranger.

"Do I have to make that extra ride?" complained the beaver man, angry again.

"Sure," answered the Ranger. "That's only a mile or so and then it's only a few more miles to the cabin, and we aren't afraid of the dark."

They watched us curiously while we hustled and scraped a pile of dead sage and grass and rubbish, and set it to smoking and made the Elks' "O. K." signal. The other Scouts must have been sweeping the horizon and hoping, for back came the "O. K." signal from them.

And traveling our fastest, with the beaver man grumbling, we all headed across the plateau for the place of the smoke. Sunday was turning out good, after all.

CHAPTER XV

GENERAL ASHLEY DROPS OUT

(JIM BRIDGER RESUMES THE TALE)

I tell you, we were glad to have that smoke of ours answered, and to see Major Henry and Kit Carson and Jed Smith coming, in the twilight, with the Ranger and the beaver man. We guessed that the three boys must be our three partners—and when they waved with the Elk Patrol sign we knew; but of course we didn't know who the two strangers were.

While they were approaching, Major Henry wigwagged: "All there?" with his cap; and Fitzpatrick wigwagged back: "Sure!" They arrived opposite us, and then headed by the man with the rifle, who was leading the horse, they obliqued up along the gulch as if they knew of a crossing; so we decided that one of the strangers must be acquainted with the country. They made a fine sight, against the horizon.

Pretty soon into the gulch they plunged, and after a few minutes out they scrambled, man and horse first, on our side, and came back toward us. And in a minute more we Elk Scouts were dancing and hugging each other, and calling each other by our regular ordinary names, "Fat" and "Sliver" and "Red" and all, and discipline didn't cut much figure. That was a joyful reunion. The Ranger and his prisoner, the beaver man, looked on.

Then when Major Henry hauled out the message packet, and saluting and grinning passed it to the general, our cup was full. I was as glad as if I had passed it, myself. "One for all, and all for one," is the way we Scouts work.

"If you hadn't trailed him (the beaver man) and headed him and fixed him so he couldn't travel fast, he'd have got away from the fire and wouldn't have run into us," claimed Major Henry.

"And if you fellows hadn't held that fire line you wouldn't have seen him and we might have been burnt or suffocated in the willows," I claimed back.

So what seems a failure or a bother, when you're trying your best, often is the most important thing of all, or helps make the chain complete.

But now we didn't take much time to explain to each other or to swap yarns; for the twilight was gone and the dark was closing in, and we weren't in the best of shape. The burro Apache was packed with bedding, mostly, which was a good thing, of course; the Red Fox Scouts had their outfit; but we Elks were short on grub. That piece of bacon and just the little other stuff carried by the Major Henry party were our provisions. Fitz and the poor general were making a hungry camp, when we had discovered them. And then there was the general, laid up.

"What's the matter with you, kid?" queried the Ranger.

"Sprained ankle, I think."

"That's sure bad," sympathized the Ranger.

And it sure was.

"Boys, I'll have to be traveling for that cabin of mine, to report about the fire and this man," said the Ranger, after listening to our talk for a minute. "If you're grub-shy, some of you had better come along and I'll send back enough to help you out."

That was mighty nice of him. And the general spoke up, weakly. "How far is the cabin, please?"

"About three miles, straight across."

"If I could make it, could I stay there a little while?"

"Stay a year, if you want to. We'll pack you over, if you'll go. Can you ride?"

"All right," said the general. "I'll do it. Now, you fellows, listen. Major Henry, I turn the command and the message over to you. I'm no good; I can't travel and we've spent a lot of time already, and I'd be only a drag. So I'll drop out and go over to that cabin, and you other Scouts take the message."

Oh, we didn't want to do that! Leave the general? Never!

"No, sir, we'll take you along if we have to carry you on our backs," we said; and we started in, all to talk at once. But he made us quit.

"Say, do I have to sit here all night while you chew the rag?" grumbled the beaver man. But we didn't pay attention to him.

"It doesn't matter about me, whether I go or not, as long as we get that message through," answered the general, to us. "I can't travel, and I'd only hold you back and delay things. I'll quit, and the rest of you hustle and make up for lost time."

"I'll stay with you. This is Scout custom: two by two," spoke up little Jed Smith. He was the general's mate.

"Nobody stays with me. You all go right on under Corporal Henry."

"It'll be plumb dark before we get to that cabin," grumbled the beaver man. "This ain't any way to treat a fellow who's been stuck and then burnt. I'm tired o' sittin' on this hoss with my toes out."

"Well, you can get off and let this other man ride. I'll hobble you and he can lead you," said the Ranger.

"What's the matter with the burro?" growled the beaver man. He wasn't so anxious to walk, after all.

Sure! We knew that the Ranger was waiting, so while some of us led up Apache, others bandaged the general's ankle tighter, to make it ride easier and not hurt so much if it dangled. Then we lifted the general, Scout fashion, on our hands, and set him on Apache.

Now something else happened. Red Fox Scout Ward stepped forward and took the lead rope.

"I'm going," he announced quietly. "I'm feeling fine and you other fellows are tired. Somebody must bring the burro back, and the general may need a hand."

"No, I won't," corrected the general.

"But the burro must come back."

"It's up to us Elk Scouts to do that," protested Major Henry. "Some of us will go. You stay. It's dark."

"No, sir. You Elk men have been traveling on short rations and Van Sant and I have been fed up. It's either Van or I, and I'll go." And he did. He was bound to. But it was a long extra tramp.

We shook hands with the general, and gave him the Scouts' cheer; and a cheer for the Ranger.

"Ain't we ever goin' to move on?" grumbled the beaver man.

"I may stay all night and be back early in the morning," called Ward.

"Of course."

They trailed away, in the dimness—the Ranger ahead leading the beaver man, Red Fox Scout Ward leading Apache. And we were sorry to see them go. We should miss the plucky Ashley, our captain.

CHAPTER XVI

A BURRO IN BED

When I woke in the morning Fitz was already up, building the fire, according to routine, and Red Fox Scout Van Sant was helping him. So I rolled out at once, and here came Red Fox Scout Ward with the burro, across the mesa, for the camp.

He brought a little flour and a few potatoes and a big hunk of meat, and a fry-pan. He brought a map of the country, too, that he had sketched from information from the Ranger. That crack beside Pilot Peak, where the sun had set, was a pass through, which we could take for Green Valley. It was a pass used by the Indians and buffalo, once, and an old Indian trail crossed it still. The general sent word that if we took that trail, he would get the goods we had left cached.

"Now," reported Major Henry, when we had filled for a long day's march, "I'll put it to vote. We can either find that cache ourselves, and take the trail from there, as first planned, or we can head straight across the mountain. It's a short cut for the other side of the range, but it may be rough traveling. The other way, beyond the cache, looked pretty rough, too. But we'd have our traps and supplies,—as much as we could pack on Apache, anyhow."

"I vote we go straight ahead, over the mountain, this way," said Fitz. "We'll get through. We've got to. We've been out seven days, and we aren't over, yet."

We counted. That was so. Whew! We must hurry. Kit and Jed and I voted with Fitz.

"All right. Break camp," ordered Major Henry.

He didn't have to speak twice.

"That Ranger says we can strike the railroad, over on the other side, Van, and make our connections there," said Red Fox Scout Ward to his partner. "Let's go with the Elks and see them through that far."

That was great. They had come off their trail a long way already, helping me, it seemed to us—but if they wanted to keep us company further, hurrah! Only, we wouldn't sponge off of them, just because they had the better outfit, now.

We policed the camp, and put out the fire, through force of habit, and with the burro packed with the squaw hitch , and the Red Foxes packed, forth we started, as the sun was rising, to follow the Ute trail, over Pilot Peak. The Red Fox Scouts carried their own stuff; they wouldn't let us put any of it on Apache, for they were independent, too.

Travel wasn't hard. After we crossed the gorge the top of the mesa or plateau was flat and gravelly, with some sage and grass, and we made good time. We missed the general, and we were sorry to leave that cache, but we had cut loose and were taking the message on once more. Thus we began our second week out.

The forest fire was about done. Just a little smoke drifted up, in the distance behind and below. But from our march we could see where the fire had passed through the timber, yonder across; and that blackened swath was a melancholy sight. We didn't stop for nooning, and when we made an early camp the crack had opened out, and was a pass, sure enough.

Red Fox Scout Van Sant and I were detailed to take the two rifles and hunt for rabbits. We got three—two cottontails and a jack—among the willows where a stream flowed down from the pass. The stream was swarming here with little trout, and Jed Smith and Kit Carson caught twenty-four in an hour. So we lived high again.

Those Red Fox Scouts had a fine outfit. They had a water-proof silk tent, with jointed poles. It folded to pocket size, and didn't weigh anything at all; but when set up it was large enough for them both to sleep in. Then they had a double sleeping bag, and blankets that were light and warm both, and a lot of condensed foods and that little alcohol stove, and a complete kit of aluminum cooking and eating ware that closed together— and everything went into those two packs.

They used the packs instead of burros or pack-horses. I believe that animals are better in the mountains where a fellow climbs at ten and twelve thousand feet, and where the nights are cold so he needs more bedding than lower down. Man-packs are all right in the flat timber and in the hills out East, I suppose. But all styles have their good points, maybe; and a Scout must adapt himself to the country. We all can't be the same.

Because the Red Fox Scouts were Easterners, clear from New Jersey, and we were Westerners, of Colorado, we sort of eyed them sideways, at first. They had such a swell outfit, you know, and their uniform was smack to the minute, while ours was rough and ready. They set up their tent, and we let them—but our way was to sleep out, under tarps (when we had tarps), in the open. We didn't know but what, on the march, they might want to keep their own mess—they had so many things that we didn't. But right away a good thing happened again.

"How did Fitzpatrick lose his arm?" asked Scout Van Sant of me, when we were out hunting and Fitz couldn't hear.

"In the April Day mine," I said.

"Where?"

"Back home."

He studied. "I thought the name of that town sounded awfully familiar to me," he said.

When we came into camp with our rabbits, he went straight up to Fitz.

"I hear you hurt your arm in the April Day mine," he said.

"Yes. I was working there," answered Fitz. "Why?"

Van Sant stuck out his hand. "Shake," he said. "My father owns that mine—or most of it. Ever hear of him?"

"No," said Fitz, flushing. "I'm just a mucker and a sorter. My father's a miner."

"Well, shake," laughed Van Sant. "I never even mucked or sorted, and you know more than I do about it. My father just owns—and if it wasn't for the workers like you and your father, the mine wouldn't be worth owning. See? I'm mighty sorry you got hurt there, though."

Fitz shook hands. "It was partly my own fault," he said. "I took a chance. That was before your father bought the mine, anyway."

Then he went to cooking and we cleaned our game. But from that time on we knew the Red Fox Scouts to be all right, and their being from the East made no difference in them. So we and they used each other's things, and we all mixed in together and were one party.

We had a good camp and a big rest, this night: the first time of real peace since a long while back, it seemed to me. The next morning we pushed on, following up along the creek, and a faint trail, for the pass.

This day's march was a hard climb, every hour, and it took our wind, afoot. But by evening old Pilot Peak wasn't far at all. His snow patches were getting larger. When we camped in a little park we must have been up about eleven thousand feet, and the breeze from the Divide ahead of us blew cool.

The march now led through aspens and pines and wild flowers, with the stream singing, and forming little waterfalls and pools and rapids, and full of those native trout about as large as your two fingers. There was the old Indian trail, to guide us. It didn't have a track except deer-tracks, and we might have been the only white persons ever here. That was fine. Another sign was the amount of game. Of course, some of the game may have been driven here by the forest fire. But we saw lots of grouse, which sat as we passed by, and rabbits and porcupines, and out of the aspens we jumped deer.

We arrived where the pretty little stream, full of songs and pictures and trout, came tumbling out of a canyon with bottom space for just it alone.

The old Indian trail obliqued off, up a slope, through the timber on the right, and so did we.

It was very quiet, here. The lumber folks had not got in with their saws and axes, and the trees were great spruces, so high and stately that we felt like ants. Among the shaded, nice-smelling aisles the old trail wound. Sometimes it was so covered with the fallen needles that we could not see it; and it had been blazed, years ago, by trappers or somebody, and where it crossed glades we came upon it again. It was an easy trail.

We reached the top of a little ridge, and before us we saw the pass. 'Twas a wide, open pass, with snow-banks showing on it, and the sun swinging down to set behind it.

The trail forked, one branch making for the pass, the other making for the right, where Pilot Peak loomed close at hand. There was some reason why the trail forked, and as we surveyed we caught the glint of a lake, over there.

Major Henry examined the sketch map. "That must be Medicine Lake," he said. "I think we'd better go over there and camp, instead of trying the pass. We're sure of wood and water, and it won't be so windy."

The trail took us safely to the brow of a little basin, and looking down we saw the lake. It was lying at the base of Pilot Peak. Above it on one side rose a steep slope of a gray slide-rock, like a railway cut, only of course no railroad was around here; and all about, on the other sides, were pointed pines.

I tell you, that was beautiful. And when we got to the lake we found it to be black as ink—only upon looking into it you could see down, as if you were looking through smoky crystal. The water was icy cold, and full of specks dancing where the sun struck, and must have been terrifically deep.

We camped beside an old log cabin, all in ruins. It was partly roofed over with sod, but we spread our beds outside; these old cabins are great places for pack-rats and skunks and other animals like those. Fish were jumping in the lake, and the two Red Fox Scouts and I were detailed to catch some. The Red Fox Scouts tried flies, but the water was as smooth as glass, and you can't fool these mountain lake-trout, very often, that way. Then we put on spinners and trolled from the shores by casting. We could see the fish, gliding sluggishly about, — great big fellows; but they never noticed our hooks, and we didn't have a single strike. So we must quit, disgusted.

The night was grand. The moon was full, and came floating up over the dark timber which we had left, to shine on us and on the black lake and on the mountain. Resting there in our blankets, we Elk Scouts could see all about us. The lake lay silent and glassy, except when now and then a big old trout plashed. The slide-rock bank gleamed white, and above it stretched the long rocky slope of Pilot, with the moon casting lights and shadows clear to its top.

This was a mighty lonely spot, up here, by the queer lake, with timber on one side and the mountain on the other; the air was frosty, because ice would form any night, so high; not a sound could be heard, save the plash of trout, or the sighs of Apache as he fidgeted and dozed and grazed; but the Red Fox Scouts were snug under their tent, and under our bedding we Elks were cuddled warm, in two pairs and with Major Henry sleeping single.

We did not need to hobble or picket Apache. He had come so far that he followed like a dog and stayed around us like a dog. When you get a burro out into the timber or desert wilds and have cut him loose from his regular stamping ground, then he won't be separated from you. He's afraid. Burros are awfully funny animals. They like company. So when we camped we just turned Apache out, and he hung about pretty close, expecting scraps of bread and stuff and enjoying our conversation.

To-night he kept snorting and fussing, and edging in on us, and before we went to sleep we had to throw sticks at him and shoo him off. It seemed too lonesome for him, up here. Then we dropped to sleep, under the moon —

and then, the first thing Fitz and I knew, Apache was trying to crawl into bed with us!

That waked us. Nobody can sleep with a burro under the same blanket. Apache was right astraddle of us and was shaking like an aspen leaf; his long ears were pricked, he was glaring about, and how he snorted! I sat up; so did Fitz. We were afraid that Apache might step on our faces.

"Get out, Apache!" we begged. But he wouldn't "get." He didn't budge, and we had to push him aside, with our hands against his stomach.

Now the whole camp was astir, grumbling and turning. Apache ran and tried to bunk with Kit and Jed. "Get out!" scolded Kit; and repulsed here, poor Apache stuck his nose in between the flaps of the silk tent and began to shove inside.

Something crackled amidst the brush along the lake, and there sounded a snort from that direction, also. It was a peculiar snort. It was a grunty, blowy snort. And beside me Fitz stiffened and lifted his head further.

"Bear!" he whispered.

"Whoof!" it answered.

"Bear! Look out! There's a bear around!" said the camp, from bed to bed.

Down came the silk tent on top of Apache, and out from under wriggled the Red Fox Scouts, as fast as they could move. Their hair was rumpled up, they were pale in the moonlight, and Van Sant had his twenty-two rifle ready. That must have startled them, to be waked by a big thing like Apache forcing a way into their tent.

"Who said bear? Where is it?" demanded Van Sant.

"Don't shoot!" ordered Major Henry, sharply, sitting up. "Don't anybody shoot. That will make things worse. Tumble out, everybody, and raise a noise. Give a yell. We can scare him."

"I see it!" cried Ward. "Look! In that clear spot yonder—up along the lake, about thirty yards."

Right! A blackish thing as big as a cow was standing out in the moonlight, facing us, its head high. We could almost see its nostrils as it sniffed.

Up we sprang, and whooped and shouted and waved and threw sticks and stones into the brush. With another tremendous "Whoof!" the bear wheeled, and went crashing through the brush as if it had a tin can tied to its tail. We all cheered and laughed.

"Jiminy! I ought to have tried a flashlight of it," exclaimed Fitz, excited. "If we see another bear I'm sure going to get its picture. I need some bear pictures. Don't let's be in such a hurry, next time."

"That depends on the bear," said little Jed Smith. "Sometimes you can't help being in a hurry, with a bear."

"Guess we'd better dig the burro out of our tent," remarked Scout Ward. "He smelled that bear, didn't he?"

He certainly did. If there's one thing a burro is afraid of, it's a bear. No wonder poor Apache tried to crawl in with us. We hauled him loose of the tent, and helped the Red Fox Scouts set the tent up again. Apache snorted and stared about; and finally he quieted a little and went to browsing, close by, and we Scouts turned in to sleep again.

When I woke the next time it was morning and the bear had not come back, for Apache was standing fast asleep in the first rays of the sun, at the edge of the camp.

We could catch no fish for breakfast. They paid no attention to any bait. So we had the last of the meat, and some condensed sausage that the Red Fox Scouts contributed to the pot. During breakfast we held a council; old Pilot Peak stuck up so near and inviting.

"I've been thinking, boys, that maybe we ought to climb Pilot, for a record, now we've got a good chance," proposed Major Henry. "What do you say. Shall we vote on it?"

"How high is it?" asked Red Fox Scout Ward.

Major Henry looked at the map of the state. "Fourteen thousand, two hundred and ten feet."

"Whew!" Scout Ward eyed it. "We'd certainly like to make it. That would be a chance for an honor, eh, Van?"

"You bet," agreed Van Sant.

"He's sure some mountain," we said.

"We haven't any time to spare from the trail," went on Major Henry, "and it would kill a day, to the top and back. So we ought to double up by traveling by night, some. But that wouldn't hurt any; it would be fun, by moonlight. Now, if you're ready, all who vote to take the Red Fox Scouts and climb old Pilot Peak for a record hold up their right hands."

"We won't vote. Don't make the climb on our account," cried the Red Fox Scouts.

"Let's do it. I've never been fourteen thousand feet, myself," declared Fitz.

And we all held up our right hands.

"Bueno," quoth Major Henry. "Then we go. We'll climb Pilot and put in extra time on the trail. Cache the stuff, police the camp, put out the fire, take what grub we can in our pockets, and the sooner we start the better."

Maybe we ought not to have done this. Our business was the message. We weren't out for fun or for honors. We were out to carry that message through in the shortest time possible. The climb was not necessary—and I for one had a sneaking hunch that we were making a mistake. But I hadvoted yes, and so had we all. If anybody had felt dubious, he ought to have voted no.

In the next chapter you will read what we got, by fooling with a side issue.

CHAPTER XVII

VAN SANT'S LAST CARTRIDGE

The way to climb a mountain is not to tackle it by the short, steep way, but to go up by zigzags, through little gulches and passes. You arrive about as quick and you arrive easier.

Now from camp we eyed Old Pilot, calculating. Major Henry pointed.

"We'll follow up that draw, first," he said. "Then we can cross over to that ledge, and wind around and hit the long stretch, where the snow patches are. After that, I believe, we can go right on up."

We had just rounded the lower end of the lake, and were obliquing off and up for the draw, when we heard a funny bawly screech behind us, and a clattering, and along at a gallop came Apache, much excited, and at a trot joined our rear. He did not propose to be left alone! We were glad enough to have him, if he wanted to make the climb, too. He followed us all the way, eating things, and gained a Scout mountain honor.

We were traveling light, of course. Fitz had his camera slung over his shoulder, Red Fox Scout Van Sant had his twenty-two rifle, because we thought we might run into some grouse, and the law on grouse was out at last and we needed meat. Nobody bothered with staffs. They're no good when you must use hands and knees all at once, as you do on some of the Rocky Mountains. They're a bother.

We struck into the draw. It was shallow and bushy, with sarvice-berries and squaw-berries and gooseberries; but we didn't stop to eat. We let Apache do the eating. Our thought was to reach the very tip-top of Pilot.

The sun shone hot, making us sweat as we followed up through the draw, in single file, Major Henry leading, Fitz next, then the Red Fox Scouts, and we three others strung out behind, with Apache closing the rear. The draw brought us out, as we had planned, opposite the ledge, and we swung off to this.

Now we were up quite high. We halted to take breath and puff. The ledge was broad and flat and grassy, with rimrock behind it; and from it we could look down upon the lake, far below, and the place of our camp, and the big timber through which we had trailed, and away in the distance was the mesa or plateau that we had crossed after the forest fire. We were above timber-line, and all around us were only sunshine and bareness, and warmth and nice clean smells.

"Whew!" sighed Red Fox Scout Ward. "It's fine, fellows."

That was enough. We knew how he felt. We felt the same.

But of course we weren't at the top, not by any means. Major Henry started again, on the upward trail. We followed along the ledge around the rimrock until we came to a little pass through. That brought us into a regular maze of big rocks, lying as if a chunk as big as a city block had dropped and smashed, scattering pieces all about. This spot didn't show from below. That is the way with mountains. They look smooth, but when you get up close they break out into hills and holes and rocks and all kinds of unexpected places, worse than measles.

But among these jagged chunks we threaded, back and forth, always trying to push ahead, until suddenly Red Fox Scout Ward called, "I'm out!" and we went to him. So he was.

That long, bare slope lay beyond, blotched with snow. The snow had not seemed much, from below; but now it was in large patches, with drifts so hard that we could walk on them. One drift was forty feet thick; it was lodged against a brow, and down its face was trickling black water, streaking it. This snow-bank away up here was the beginning of a river, and helped make the lake.

We had spread out, with Apache still behind. Suddenly little Jed called. "See the chickens?" he said.

We went over. Chirps were to be heard, and there among the drifts, on the gravelly slope, were running and pecking and squatting a lot of birds about like gray speckled Brahmas. They were as tame as speckled Brahmas, too. They had red eyes and whitish tails.

"Ptarmigan!" exclaimed Fitz, and he began to take pictures. He got some first-class ones.

Red Fox Scout Van Sant never made a move to shoot any of them. They were so tame and barn-yardy. We were glad enough to let them live, away up here among the snowdrifts, where they seemed to like to be. It was their country, not ours—and they were plucky, to choose it. So we passed on.

The slope brought us up to a wide moraine, I guess you'd call it, where great bowlders were heaped as thick as pebbles—bowlders and blocks as large as cottages. These had not looked to be much, either, from below.

On the edge of them we halted, to look down and behind again. Now we were much higher. The ledge was small and far, and the timber was small and farther, and the world was beginning to lie flat like a map. On the level with us were only a few other peaks, in the snowy Medicine Range. Thepass itself was so low that we could scarcely make it out.

To cross that bowlder moraine was a terrific job. We climbed and sprawled, and were now up, now down. It was a go-as-you-please. Everywhere among the bowlders were whistling rock-rabbits, or conies. They were about the size of small guinea-pigs, and had short tails and round, flat bat ears plastered close to their heads. They had their mouths crammed full of dried grass, which they carried into their nests through crannies—putting away hay for the winter! It was mighty cheerful to have them so busy and greeting us, away up in these lonely heights, and Fitz got some more good animal pictures.

Apache was in great distress. He couldn't navigate those bowlders. We could hear him "hee-hawing" on the lower edge, and could see him staring after us and racing frantically back and forth. But we must go on; we would pick him up on our way down.

Well, we got over the bowlder field—Fitz as spryly as any of us. Having only one good arm made no difference to him, and he never would accept help. He was independent, and we only kept an eye on him and let him alone. The bowlders petered out; and now ahead was another slope, with more snow patches, and short dead grass in little bunches; and it ended in a bare outcrop: the top!

Our feet weighed twenty-five pounds each, our knees were wobbly, we could hear each other pant, and my heart thumped so that the beats all ran together. But with a cheer we toiled hard for the summit, before resting. We didn't race—not at fourteen thousand feet; we weren't so foolish—and I don't know who reached it first. Anyway, soon we all were there.

We had climbed old Pilot Peak! The top was flat and warm and dry, so we could sit. The sky was close above; around about was nothing but the clear air. East, west, north and south, below us, were hills and valleys and timber and parks and streams, with the cloud-shadows drifting across. We didn't say one word. The right words didn't exist, somehow, and what was the use in exclaiming when we all felt alike, and could look and see for ourselves? You don't seem to amount to much when you are up, like this, on a mountain, near the sky, with the world spread out below and not missing you; and a boy's voice, or a man's, is about the size of a cricket's chirp. The silence is one of the best things you find. So we sat and looked and thought.

But on a sudden we did hear a noise—a rattling and "Hee-haw!" And here, from a different side, came Apache again. He had got past thosebowlders, somehow. With another "Hee-haw!" he trotted right up on top, in amidst us, where he stood, with a big sigh, looking around, too.

This was the chance for us to map out the country ahead, on the other side of the pass. So we took a good long survey. It was a rough country, as bad as that which we had left; with much timber and many hills and valleys. Down in some of the valleys were yellow patches, like hay ranches, and forty or fifty miles away seemed to be a little haze of smoke, which must be a town: Green Valley, where we were bound! Hurrah! But we hadn't got there, yet.

Major Henry made a rough sketch of the country, with Pilot Peak as base point and a jagged, reddish tip, over toward the smoke, as another landmark. Our course ought to be due west from Pilot, keeping to the south of that reddish tip.

We had a little lunch, and after cleaning up after ourselves we saluted the old peak with the Scouts' cheer, saying good-by to it; and then we started down. We discovered that we could go around the bowlder-field, as Apache had done. When we struck the snow-patch slope we obliqued over to our trail up, and began to back track. Back-tracking was the safe way, because we knew that this would bring us out. Down we went, with long steps, almost flying, and leaving behind us the busy conies and the tame ptarmigans, to inhabit the peak until we should come again. We even tried not to tramp on the flowers.

Through the maze of rock masses we threaded, and along the grassy ledge, and entered the bush draw. By the sun it was noon, but we had plenty of time, and we spread out in the draw, taking things easy and picking berries. We didn't know but what we might come upon some grouse, in here, too, for the trickle from that snow-bank drained through and there was a bunch of aspens toward the bottom. But instead we came upon a bear!

I heard Red Fox Scout Ward call, sharp and excited: "Look out, fellows! Here's another bear!"

That stopped us short.

"Where?"

"Right in front of me! He's eating berries. And I see another, too—sitting, looking at me."

"Wait!" called back Fitz, excited. "Let 'em alone. I'll get a picture."

That was just like Fitzpatrick. He wanted to take pictures of everything alive.

"Yes; let 'em alone," warned Major Henry, shouting.

For that's all a bear in a berry-patch asks; to be let alone. He's satisfied with the berries. In fact, all a bear asks, anyway, is to be let alone, and up here on the mountain these bears weren't doing any harm.

"Where are you?" called Fitz.

"On this rock."

Now we could see Scout Ward, with hand up; and over hustled Fitz, and over we all hustled, from different directions.

They were not large bears. They looked like the little brown or black bears, it was hard to tell which; but the small kind isn't dangerous. They were across on the edge of a clearing, and were stripping the bushes. Once in a while they would sit up and eye us, while slobbering down the berries; then they would go to eating again.

Fitz had his camera unslung and taken down. He walked right out, toward them, and snapped, but it wouldn't be a very good picture. They were too far to show up plainly.

"I'll sneak around behind and drive them out," volunteered little Jed Smith; and without waiting for orders he and Kit started, and we all except Fitz spread out to help in the surround. Fitz made ready to take them on the run. Nobody is afraid of the little brown or black bear.

Jed and Kit were just entering the bushes to make the circuit on their side, when we heard Apache snorting and galloping, and a roar and a "Whoof!" and out from the brush over there burst the burro, with another bear chasing him. This was no little bear. It was a great big bear — an old she cinnamon, and these others weren't the small brown or black bears, either: they were half-grown cinnamon cubs!

How she came! Kit Carson and Jed Smith were right in her path.

"Look out!" we yelled.

Kit and little Jed leaped to dodge. She struck like a cat as she passed, and head over heels went poor little Jed, sprawling in the brush, and she passed on, straight to her cubs. They met her, and she smelled them for a moment. She lifted her broad, short head, and snarled.

"Don't do a thing," ordered Major Henry. "She'll leave."

So we stood stock-still. That was all we could do. We knew that poor little Jed was lying perhaps badly wounded, off there in the brush, but it wouldn't help to call the old bear's attention to him again. In the open place Fitzpatrick the Bad Hand stood; he was right in front of the old bear, and he was taking pictures!

The old bear saw him, and he and the camera seemed to make her mad. Maybe she took it for a weapon. She lowered her head, swung it to and fro, her bristles rose still higher, and across the open space she started.

"Fitz!" we shrieked. And I said to myself, sort of crying: "Oh, jiminy!"

We all set up a tremendous yell, but that didn't turn her. Major Henry jumped forward, and tugged to pull loose a stone. I looked for a stone to throw. Of course I couldn't find one. Then out of the corner of my eye, while I was watching Fitz, too, I glimpsed Red Fox Scout Van Sant coming running, and shooting with his twenty-two. The bullets spatted into the bear's hide, and stung her.

"Run, Fitz!" called Van Sant. "I'll stop her."

But he didn't, yet. Hardly! That Fitz had just been winding his film. He took the camera from between his knees, where he had held it while he used his one hand, and he leveled it like lightning, on the old bear—and took her picture again. That picture won a prize, after we got back to civilization. But the old bear kept coming.

We all were shouting, in vain,—shouting all kinds of things. Red Fox Scout Van Sant sprang to Fitz's side, and again we heard him say: "Run, Fitz! Over here. Make for the rock. I'll stop her."

It was the outcrop where Ward had been. Fitz jumped to make for it. He hugged his camera as he ran. We thought that Van Sant would make for it, too. But he let Fitz pass him, and he stood. The old bear was coming, crazy. She only halted to scratch where a twenty-two pellet had stung her hide. Van Sant waited, steady as a rock. He lifted his little rifle slowly and held on her, and just as she was about to reach him he fired.

"Crack!"

Headfirst she plunged. She kicked and ripped the ground, and didn't get up again. She lay still, amidst a silence, we all watching, breathless. Beyond, Fitzpatrick had closed his precious camera as he ran, and now at the rock had turned.

"Shoot her again, Van!" begged Scout Ward.

"I can't," he answered. "That was my last cartridge. But she's dead. I hit her in the eye." And he lowered his rifle.

Then we gave a great cheer, and rushed for the spot—except Major Henry; he was the first to think and he rushed to see to little Jed Smith. Fitzpatrick shook hands hard with Red Fox Scout Van Sant and followed the major.

Yes, the old bear was stone dead. Van Sant had shot her through the eye, into the brain. That was enough. Ward and I shook hands with him, too. He had shown true Scouts' nerve, to sail in in that way, and to meet the danger and to be steady under fire.

"Oh, well, I was the only one who could do anything," he explained. "I knew it was my last cartridge and I had to make it count. That's all."

Then we hurried down to where the Major and Fitz and Kit Carson were gathered about little Jed. Jed wasn't dead. No; we could see him move. And Fitz called: "He's all right. But his shoulder's out and his leg is torn."

Little Jed was pale but game. His right arm hung dangling and useless, and his right calf was bloody. The whole arm hung dangling because the shoulder was hurt; but it was not a fractured collarbone, for when we had laid open Jed's shirt we could feel and see. The shoulder was out of shape, and commencing to swell, and the arm hung lower than the well arm.

We let the wound of the calf go, for we must get at this dislocation, before the shoulder was too sore and rigid. We knew what to do. Jed was stretched on his back, Red Fox Scout Ward sat at his head, steadying him around the body, and with his stockinged heel under Jed's armpit Major Henry pulled down on the arm and shoved up against it with his heel at the same time. That hurt. Jed turned very white, and let out a big grunt — but we heard a fine snap, and we knew that the head of the arm-bone had chucked back into the shoulder-socket where it belonged.

So that was over; and we were glad, — Jed especially. We bound his arm with a handkerchief sling across to the other shoulder, to keep the joint in place for a while, and we went at his leg.

The old bear's paw had cuffed him on the shoulder and then must have slipped down and landed on his calf as he sprawled. The boot-top had been ripped open and the claws had cut through into the flesh, tearing a set of furrows. It was a bad-looking wound and was bleeding like everything. But the blood was just the ordinary oozy kind, and so we let it come, to clean the wound well. Then we laid some sterilized gauze from our first-aid outfit upon it, to help clot the blood, and sifted borax over, and bound it tight with adhesive plaster, holding the edges of the furrows together. Over that we bound on loosely a dry pack of other gauze.

We left Jed (who was pale but thankful) with Red Fox Scout Ward and went up to the bear. Kit Carson wanted to see her. She was still dead, and off on the edge of the brush her two cubs were sniffing in her direction, wondering and trying to find out.

Yes, that had been a nervy stand made by Scout Van Sant, and a good shot. Fitzpatrick reached across and shook his hand again.

"I don't know whether I stopped to thank you, but it's worth doing twice. I'm much obliged."

"Don't mention it," laughed Van Sant.

Then we all laughed. That was better. There isn't much that can be said, when you feel a whole lot. But you know, just the same. And we all were Scouts.

Somehow, the big limp body of the old mother bear now made us sober. We hadn't intended to kill her, and of course she was only protecting her cubs. It wasn't our mountain; and it wasn't our berry-patch. She had discovered it first. We had intruded on her, not she on us. It all was a misunderstanding.

So we didn't gloat over her, or kick her, or sit upon her, now that she could not defend herself. But we must do some quick thinking.

"Kit Carson, you and Bridger catch Apache," ordered Major Henry. "Fitz and I will help Scout Van Sant skin his bear."

"She's not my bear," said Scout Van Sant. "I won't take her. She belongs to all of us."

"Well," continued Major Henry, "it's a pity just to let her lie and to waste her. We can use the meat."

"The pelt's no good, is it?" asked Fitz.

"Not much, in the summer. But we'll take it off, and put the meat in it, to carry."

They set to work. Kit Carson and I started after the burro. He had run off, up the mountain again, and we couldn't catch him. He was too nervous. We'd get close to him, and with a snort and a toss of his ears he would jump away and fool us. That was very aggravating.

"If we only had a rope we could rope him," said Kit. But we didn't. There was no profit in chasing a burro all over a mountain, and so, hot and tired, we went back and reported.

The old bear had been skinned and butchered, after a fashion. The head was left on the hide, for the brains. At first Major Henry talked of sending down to camp for a blanket and making a litter out of it. We would have hard work to carry Jed in our arms. But Jed was weak and sick and didn't want to wait for the blanket. Apache would have been a big help, only he was so foolish. But we had a scheme. Scouts always manage.

We made a litter of the bear-pelt! Down we scurried to the aspens and found two dead sticks. We stuck one through holes in the pelt's fore legs, and one through holes in the pelt's hind legs, and tied the legs about with cord. We set little Jed in the hair side, facing the bear's head, turned back over; the Major, the two Red Fox Scouts, and Kit Carson took each an end of the sticks; Fitzpatrick and I carried the meat, stuck on sticks, over our shoulders; and in a procession like cave-men or trappers returning from a hunt we descended the mountain, leaving death and blood where we had intended to leave only peace as we had found it.

Apache made a big circuit to follow us. The two cubs sneaked forward, to sniff at the bones where their mother had been cut up—and began to eat her. We were glad to know that they did not feel badly yet, and that they were old enough to take care of themselves.

But as we stumbled and tugged, carrying wounded Jed down the draw, we knew plainly that we ought to have let that mountain alone.

CHAPTER XVIII

FITZ THE BAD HAND'S GOOD THROW

That green bear-pelt and Jed together were almost too heavy, so that we went slow and careful and stopped often, to rest us. The sun was setting when at last we got down to camp again—and we arrived, a very different party from that which had gone out twelve hours before. It was a sorry home-coming. But we must not lament or complain over what was our own fault. We must do our best to turn it to account. We must be Scouts.

We made Jed comfortable on a blanket bed. His leg we let alone, as the bandage seemed to be all right. And his shoulder we of course let alone. Then we took stock. Major Henry decided very quickly.

"Jed can't travel. He will have to stay here till his wounds heal more, and Kit Carson will have to stay with him. I'd stay, instead, because I'm to blame for wasting some men and some time; but the general passed the command on to me and I ought to go as far as I possibly can. We'll fix Kit and Jed the best we're able, and to-morrow we'll hustle on and make night marches, if we need to."

This was sense. Anyway, although we had wasted men and time, we were now stocked up with provisions; all that bear meat! While Fitzpatrick and Red Fox Scout Ward were cooking supper and poor Jed looked on, two of us went at the meat to cut it into strips for jerking, and two of us stretched the pelt to grain it before it dried.

We cut the meat into the strips and piled them until we could string them to smoke and dry them. We then washed for supper, because we were pretty bloody with the work of cutting. After supper, by moonlight, we strung the strips with a sailor's needle and cord which the Red Fox Scouts had in their kit, and erected a scaffolding of four fork-sticks with two other sticks laid across at the ends. We stretched the strings of meat in lines, back and forth. Next thing was to make a smudge under and to lay a tarp over to hold the smudge while the meat should smoke.

Pine smoke is no good, because it is so strong. Alder makes a fine sweet smoke, but we didn't have any alder, up here. We used aspen, as the next best thing at hand. And by the time we had the pelt grained and the meat strung and had toted enough aspen, we were tired.

But somebody must stay awake, to tend to Jed and give him a drink and keep him company, and to watch the smudge, that it didn't flame up too fierce and that it didn't go out. By smoking and drying the meat all night and by drying it in the sun afterward, Major Henry thought that it would be ready so that we could take our share along with us.

If we had that, then we would not need to stop to hunt, and we could make short camps, as we pleased. You see, we had only four days in which to deliver the message; and we had just reached the pass!

This was a kind of miserable night. Jed of course had a bed to himself, which used up blankets. The others of us stood watch an hour and a half each, over him and over the smudge. He was awful restless, because his leg hurt like sixty, and none of us slept very well, after the excitement. I was sleepiest when the time came for us to get up.

We had breakfast, of bear steak and bread or biscuits and gravy. The meat we were jerking seemed to have been smoked splendidly. The tarp was smoked, anyhow. We took it off and aired it, and left the strips as they were, to dry some more in the sun. They were dark, and quite stiff and hard, and by noon they were brittle as old leather. The hide was dry, too, and ready for working over with brains and water, and for smoking.

But we left that to Kit. Now we must take the trail again. We spent the morning fussing, and making the cabin tight for Jed and Kit; at last the meat had been jerked so that our share would keep, and we had done all that we could, and we were in shape to carry the message on over the pass and down to Green Valley.

"All right," spoke Major Henry, after dinner. "Let's be off. Scout Carson, we leave Scout Smith in your charge. You and he stay right here until he's able to travel. Then you can follow over the pass and hit Green Valley, or you can back-track for the Ranger's cabin and for home. Apache will come in soon and you'll have him to pack out with. You'll be entitled to just as much honor by bringing Jed out safe as we will by carrying the message. Isn't that so, boys?"

"Sure," we said.

But naturally Kit hated to stay behind. Only, somebody must; it was Scouts' duty. We all shook hands with him and with wounded Jed (who hated staying, too), and said "Adios," and started off.

Apache had not appeared, and we were to pack our own outfit. We left Jed and Kit enough meat and all the flour (which wasn't much) and what other stuff we could spare (they had the bearskin to use for bedding as soon as it was tanned) and one rope and our twenty-two rifle, and the Ranger's fry-pan and two cups, and we divided among us what we could carry.

"Now we've got three days and a half to get through in," announced Major Henry. We counted the days on the trail to make sure. Yes, three days and a half. "And besides, these Red Fox Scouts must catch a train in time to make connections for that Yellowstone trip. We've put in too much time, and I think we ought to travel by night as well as by day, for a while."

"Short sleeps and long marches; that's my vote," said Fitz.

"Don't do it on our account," put in the Red Fox Scouts. "But we're game. We'll travel as fast as you want to."

So we decided. And now only three Elk Scouts, instead of six, and two Red Fox Scouts, again we took the long trail. In the Ranger's cabin behind was our gallant leader General Ashley, and in this other cabin by the lake were Jed Smith and Kit Carson. Thus our ranks were being thinned.

We followed the trail from the lake and struck the old Indian trail again, leading over the pass. About the middle of the afternoon we were at the pass itself. It was wide and smooth and open and covered with gravel and short grass and little low flowers like daisies. On either side were brownish red jagged peaks and rimrock faces, specked with snow. The wind blew strong and cold. There were many sheep-tracks, where bands had been trailed over, for the low country or for the summer range. It was a wild, desolate region, with nothing moving except ourselves and a big hawk high above; but we pressed on fast, in close order, our packs on our backs, Major Henry leading. And we were lonesome without Kit and Jed.

Old Pilot Peak gradually sank behind us; the country before began to spread out into timber and meadow and valley. Pretty soon we caught up with a little stream. It flowed in the same direction that we were going, and we knew that we were across the pass and that we were on the other side of the Medicine Range, at last! Hurrah!

We were stepping long, down-hill. We came to dwarf cedars, and buck brush, showing that we were getting lower. And at a sudden halt by the major, in a nice golden twilight we threw off our packs and halted for supper beside the stream, among some aspens — the first ones.

About an hour after sunset the moon rose, opposite — a big round moon, lighting everything so that travel would be easy. We had stocked up on the jerked bear-meat, roasted on sharp sticks, and on coffee from the cubes that the Red Fox Scouts carried, and we were ready. The jerked bear-meat was fine and made us feel strong. So now Major Henry stood, and swung his pack; and we all stood.

"Let's hike," he said.

That was a beautiful march. The air was crisp and quiet, the moon mounted higher, flooding the country with silver. Once in a while a coyote barked. The rabbits all were out, hopping in the shine and shadow. We saw a snowshoe kind, with its big hairy feet. We saw several porcupines, and an owl as large as a buzzard. This was a different world from that of day, and it seemed to us that people miss a lot of things by sleeping.

Our course was due west, by the North Star. We were down off the pass, and had struck a valley, with meadow and scattered pines, and a stream rippling through, and the moonlight lying white and still. In about three hours we came upon sign of another camp, where somebody had stopped and had made a fire and had eaten. There were burro tracks here, so that it might have been a prospectors' camp; and there was an empty tin can like a large coffee can.

"I think we had better rest again," said Major Henry. "We can have a snack and a short sleep."

We didn't cook any meat. We weren't going to take out any of the Red Fox dishes, but Fitz started to fill the tin can with water, to make soup in that. It was Red Fox Scout Ward who warned us.

"Here," he objected. "Do you think we ought to do that? You know sometimes a tin can gives off poison when you cook in it."

"And we don't know what was in this can," added Van Sant. "We don't want to get ptomaine poisoning. I'd rather unpack ten packs than run any risk."

That was sense. The can looked clean, inside, and the idea of being made sick by it hadn't occurred to us Elks. But we remembered, now, some things that we'd read. So we kicked the can to one side, that nobody else should use it, and Fitz made the soup in a regulation dish from the Red Fox aluminum kit.

We drank the soup and each chewed a slice of the bear-meat cold. It was sweet and good, and the soup helped out. Then we rolled in our blankets and went to sleep. We all had it on our minds to wake in four hours, and the mind is a regular clock if you train it.

I woke just about right, according to the stars. The two stars in the bottom of the Little Dipper, that we used for an hour hand, had been exactly above a pointed spruce, when I had dozed off, and now when I looked they had moved about three feet around the Pole Star. While I lay blinking and warm and comfortable, and not thinking of anything in particular, I heard a crackle of sticks and the scratch of a match. And there squatting on the edge of a shadow was somebody already up and making a fire.

"Is that you, Fitz?" asked Major Henry.

"Yes. You fellows lie still a few seconds longer and I'll have some tea for you."

Good old Fitz! He need not have done that. He had not been ordered to. But it was a thoughtful Scout act—and was a Fitz act, to boot.

Scouts Ward and Van Sant were awake now; and we all lay watching Fitz, and waiting, as he had asked us to. Then when we saw him put in the tea—

"Levez!" spoke Major Henry; which is the old trapper custom. "Levez! Get up!"

Up we sprang, into the cold, and with our blankets about our shoulders, Indian fashion, we each drank a good swig of hot tea. Then we washed our faces, and packed our blankets, and took the trail.

It was about three in the morning. The moon was halfway down the west, and the air was chill and had that peculiar feel of just before morning. Everything was ghostly, as we slipped along, but a few birds were twittering sleepily. Once a coyote crossed our path—stopped to look back at us, and trotted away again.

Gradually the east began to pale; there were fewer stars along that horizon than along the horizon where the moon was setting. The burro tracks were plain before us, in the trail that led down the valley. The trail inclined off to the left, or to the south of west; but we concluded to follow it because we could make better time and we believed that the railroad lay in that direction. The Red Fox Scouts ought to be taken as near to the railroad as possible, before we left them. They had been mighty good to us.

The moon sank, soon the sun would be up; the birds were moving as well as chirping, the east was brightening, and already the tip of Pilot Peak, far away behind us with Kit and Jed sleeping at his base, was touched with pink, when we came upon a camp.

Red Fox Scout Van Sant, who was leading, suddenly stopped short and lifted his hand in warning. Before, in a bend of the stream that we were skirting, among the pines and spruces beside it was a lean-to, with a blackened fire, and two figures rolled in blankets; and back from the stream a little way, across in an open grassy spot, was a burro. It had been grazing, but now it was eying us with head and ears up. Red Fox Scout Van had sighted the burro first and next, of course, the lean-to camp.

We stood stock-still, surveying.

"Cache!" whispered Major Henry (which means "Hide"); and we stepped softly aside into the brush. For that burro looked very much like Sally, who had been taken from us by the two recruits when they had stolen Apache also—and by the way that the figures were lying, under a lean-to, they might be the renegade recruits themselves. It was a hostile camp!

"What is it?" whispered Red Fox Scout Ward, his eyes sparkling. "Enemy?"

"I think so," murmured Major Henry.

"We can pass."

"Sure. But if that's our burro we ought to take her." And the major explained.

The Red Foxes nodded.

"But if she isn't, then we don't want her. One of us ought to reconnoiter." And the major hesitated. "Fitz, you go," he said. And this rather surprised me, because naturally the major ought to have gone himself, he being the leader. "I've got a side-ache, somehow," he added, apologizing. "It isn't much—but it might interfere with my crawling."

Fitz was only too ready to do the stalking. He left his pack, and with a détour began sneaking upon the lean-to. We watched, breathless. But the figures never stirred. Fitz came out, opposite, and from bush to bush and tree to tree he crept nearer and nearer, with little darts from cover to cover; and at last very cautiously, on his hands and knees; and finally wriggling on his belly like a snake.

'Twas fine stalking, and we were glad that the Red Fox Scouts were here to see. But it seemed to us that Fitz was getting too near. However, the figures did not move, and did not know—and now Fitz was almost upon them. From behind a tree only a yard away from them he stretched his neck and peered, for half a minute. Then he crawled backward, and disappeared. Presently he was with us again.

"It's they, sir," he reported. "Bat and Walt. They're asleep. And that is Sally, I'm certain. I know her by the white spot on her back."

"We must have her," said the major. "She's ours. We'll get her and pack her, so we can travel better."

"Can we catch her, all right?" queried Red Fox Scout Van Sant. "We're liable to wake those two fellows up, aren't we?"

"What if we do?" put in his partner, Scout Ward. "Three of us can guard them, and the other two can chase the burro."

"No," said Major Henry. "I think we can rope her and be off before those renegades know anything about it. Can you, Fitz?"

Fitz nodded, eager.

"Then take the rope, and go after her."

Fitz did. He was a boss roper, too. You wouldn't believe it, of a one-armed boy, but it was so. All we Elk Scouts could throw a rope some. A rope comes in pretty handy, at times. Most range horses have to be caught in the corral with a rope, and knowing how to throw a rope will pull a man out of a stream or out of a hole and will perhaps save his life. But Fitz was our prize roper, because he had practiced harder than any of us, to make up for having only one arm.

The way he did was to carry the coil on his stump, and the lash end in his teeth; and when he had cast, quick as lightning he took the end from between his teeth ready to haul on it.

Major Henry might have gone, himself, to get the credit and to show what he could do; but he showed his sense by resigning in favor of Fitz.

So now at the command Fitz took the rope from him and shook it out and re-coiled it nicely. Then, carrying it, he sneaked through the trees, and crossed the creek, farther up, wading to his ankles, and advanced upon Sally.

Sally divided her attention between him and us, and finally pricked her ears at him alone. She knew what was being tried.

Coming out into the open space Fitz advanced slower and slower, step by step. He had his rope ready — the coil was on his stump, and the lash end was in his teeth, and the noose trailed by his side, from his good hand. We glanced from him and Sally to the lean-to, and back again, for the campers were sleeping peacefully. If only they would not wake and spoil matters.

Sally held her head high, suspicious and interested. Fitz did not dare to speak to her; he must trust that she would give him a chance at her before she escaped into the trees where roping would be a great deal harder.

We watched. My heart beat so that it hurt. Having that burro meant a lot to us, for those packs were heavy — and it was a point of honor, too, that we recapture our own. Here was our chance.

Fitz continued to trail his noose. He didn't swing it. Sally watched him, and we watched them both. He was almost close enough, was Fitz, to throw. A few steps more, and something would happen. But Sally concluded not to wait. She tossed her head, and with a snort turned to trot away. And suddenly Fitz, in a little run and a jerk, threw with all his might.

Straight and swift the noose sailed out, opening into an "O," and dragging the rope like a tail behind it. Fitz had grabbed the lash end from between his teeth, and was running forward, to make the cast cover more ground. It was a beautiful noose and well aimed. Before it landed we saw that it was going to land right. Just as it fell Sally trotted square into it, and it dropped over her head. She stopped short and cringed, but she was too late. Fitz had sprung back and had hauled hard. It drew tight about her neck, and she was caught. She knew it, and she stood still, with an inquiring gaze around. She knew better than to run on the rope and risk being thrown or choked. Hurrah! We would have cheered—but we didn't dare. We only shook hands all round and grinned; and in a minute came Fitz, leading her to us. She was meek enough, but she didn't seem particularly glad to seeus. We patted Fitz on the back and let him know that we appreciated him.

He had only the one throw, but that had been enough. It was like Van's last cartridge.

CHAPTER XIX

MAJOR HENRY SAYS "OUCH"

The sun was just peeping above the Medicine Range that we had crossed, when we led Sally away, back through the brush and around to strike the trail beyond the lean-to camp. After we had gone about half a mile Major Henry posted me as a rear-guard sentry, to watch the trail, and he and the other Scouts continued on until it was safe to stop and pack the burro.

The two renegade recruits did not appear. Probably they were still sleeping, with the blankets over their faces to keep out the light! In about half an hour I was signaled to come on, and when I joined the party Sally had been packed with the squaw hitch and now we could travel light again. I tell you, it was a big relief to get those loads transferred to Sally. Even the Red Foxes were glad to be rid of theirs.

Things looked bright. We were over the range; we had this stroke of luck, in running right upon Sally; the trail was fair; and the way seemed open. It wouldn't be many hours now before the Red Fox Scouts could branch off for the railroad, and get aboard a train so as to make Salt Lake in time to connect with their party for the grand trip, and we Elks had three days yet in which to deliver the message to the Mayor of Green Valley.

For two or three hours we traveled as fast as we could, driving Sally and stepping on her tracks so as to cover them. We felt so good over our prospects—over being upon the open way and winning out at last—that we struck up songs:

"Oh, the Elk is our Medicine;

He makes us very strong—"

for us; and:

"Oh, the Red fox is our Medicine—"

for the Red Fox Scouts. And we sang:

"It's honor Flag and Country dear,

and hold them in the van;

It's keep your lungs and conscience clean,

your body spick and span;

It's 'shoulders squared,' and 'be prepared,'

and always 'play the man':

Shouting the Boy Scouts forev-er!

Hurrah! Hurrah! For we're the B. S. A.!

Hurrah! Hurrah! We're ready, night and day!

You'll find us in the city street and on the open way!

Shouting the Boy Scouts forev-er!"

But at the beginning of the second verse Major Henry suddenly quit and sat down upon a log, where the trail wound through some timber. "I've got to stop a minute, boys," he gasped. "Go ahead. I'll catch up with you."

But of course we didn't. His face was white and wet, his lips were pressed tight as he breathed hard through his nose, and he doubled forward.

"What's the matter?"

"I seem to have a regular dickens of a stomach-ache," he grunted. "Almost makes me sick."

That was serious, when Major Henry gave in this way. We remembered that back on the trail when we had sighted Sally he had spoken of a "side-ache" and had sent Fitzpatrick to do the reconnoitering; but he had not spoken of it again and here we had been traveling fast with never a whimper from him. We had supposed that his side-ache was done. Instead, it had been getting worse.

"Maybe you'd better lie flat," suggested Red Fox Scout Ward. "Or try lying on your side."

"I'll be all right in a minute," insisted the major.

"We can all move off the trail, and have breakfast," proposed Fitz. "That will give him a chance to rest. We ought to have something to eat, anyway."

So we moved back from the trail, around a bend of the creek. The major could scarcely walk, he was so doubled over with cramps; Scout Ward and I stayed by to help him. But there was not much that we could do, in such a case. He leaned on us some, and that was all.

He tried lying on his side, while we unpacked Sally; and then we got him upon a blanket, with a roll for a pillow. Red Fox Scout Van Sant hustled to the creek with a cup, and fixed up a dose.

"Here," he said to the major, "swallow this."

"What is it?"

"Ginger. It ought to fix you out."

So it ought. The major swallowed it—and it was so hot it made the tears come into his eyes. In a moment he thought that he did feel better, and we were glad. We went ahead with breakfast, but he didn't eat anything, which was wise. A crampy stomach won't digest food and then you are worse.

We didn't hurry him, after breakfast. We knew that as soon as he could travel, he would. But we found that his feeling better wasn't lasting. Now that the burning of the ginger had worn off, he was as bad as ever. We were mighty sorry for him, as he turned and twisted, trying to find an easier position. A stomach-ache like that must have been is surely hard to stand.

Fitz got busy. Fitzpatrick is pretty good at doctoring. He wants to be a doctor, some day. And the Red Fox Scouts knew considerable about first-aids and simple Scouts' remedies.

"What kind of an ache is it, Tom?" queried Fitz. We were too bothered to call him "Major." "Sharp? Or steady?"

"It's a throbby ache. Keeps right at the job, though," grunted the major.

"Where?"

"Here." And the major pointed to the pit of his stomach, below the breast-bone. "It's a funny ache, too. I can't seem to strike any position that it likes."

"It isn't sour and burning, is it?" asked Red Fox Scout Ward.

"Uh uh. It's a green-apple ache, or as if I'd swallowed a corner of a brick."

We had to laugh. Still, that ache wasn't any laughing matter.

"Do you feel sick?"

"Just from the pain."

"We all ate the same, and we didn't drink out of that tin can, so it can't be poison, and it doesn't sound like just indigestion," mused Fitz to us. "Maybe we ought to give him an emetic. Shall we, Tom?"

"I don't think I need any emetic. There's nothing there," groaned the major. "Maybe I've caught cold. I guess the cramps will quit. Wish I had a hot-water bag or a hot brick."

"We'll heat water and lay a hot compress on. That will help," spoke Red Fox Scout Van Sant. "Ought to have thought of it before."

"Wait a minute, boys," bade Fitz. "Lie still as long as you can, Tom, while I feel you."

He unbuttoned the major's shirt (the major had taken off his belt and loosened his waist-band, already) and began to explore about with his fingers.

"The ache's up here," explained the major. "Up in the middle of my stomach."

"But is it sore anywhere else?" asked Fitz, pressing about. "Say ouch."

The major said ouch.

"Sore right under there?" queried Fitz.

The major nodded.

We noted where Fitz was pressing with his fingers—and suddenly it flashed across me what he was finding out. The ache was in the pit of the stomach, but the sore spot was lower and down toward the right hip.

Fitz experimented here and there, not pressing very hard; and he always could make the major say ouch, for the one spot.

"I believe he's got appendicitis," announced Fitz, gazing up at us.

"It looks that way, sure," agreed Red Fox Scout Van Sant. "My brother had appendicitis, and that's how they went to work on him."

"My father had it, is how I knew about it," explained Fitz.

"Aw, thunder!" grunted the major. "It's just a stomach-ache." He hated to be fussed with. "I'll get over it. A hot-water bag is all I need."

"No, you don't," spoke Fitz, quickly—as Red Fox Scout Ward was stirring the fire. "Hot water would be dangerous, and if it's appendicitis we shan't take any risks. They use an ice-pack in appendicitis. We'll put on cold water instead of hot, and I'm going to give him a good stiff dose of Epsom salts. I'm afraid to give him anything else."

That sounded like sense, except that the cold water instead of the hot was something new. And it was queer that if the major's appendix was what caused the trouble the ache should be off in the middle of his stomach. But Fitz was certain that he was right, and so we went ahead. The treatment wasn't the kind to do any harm, even if we were wrong in the theory. The Epsom salts would clean out most disturbances, and help reduce any inflammation.

The major was suffering badly. To help relieve him, we discussed which was worse, tooth-ache or stomach-ache. The Red Foxes took the tooth-ache side and we Elks the stomach-ache side; and we won, because the major put in his grunts for the stomach-ache. We piled a wet pack of handkerchiefs and gauze on his stomach, over the right lower angle, where the appendix ought to be; and we changed it before it got warmed. The water from the creek was icy cold. We kept at it, and after a while the major was feeling much better.

And now he began to chafe because he was delaying the march. It was almost noon. The two renegade recruits had not come along yet. They might not come at all; they might be looking around for Sally, without sense enough to read the sign. But the major was anxious to be pushing on again.

"I don't think you ought to," objected Fitz.

"But I'm all right."

"You may not be, if you stir around much," said Red Fox Scout Ward.

"What do you want me to do? Lie here for the rest of my life?" The major was cross.

"No; but you ought to be carried some place where you can have a doctor, if it's appendicitis."

"I don't believe it is. It's just a sort of colic. I'm all right now, if we go slowly."

"But don't you think that we'd better find some place where we can take you?" asked Fitz.

"You fellows leave me, then, and go on. Somebody will come along, or I'll follow slow. Those Red Foxes must get to their train, and you two Elks must carry the message through on time."

"Not much!" exclaimed both the Red Foxes, indignant. "What kind of Scouts do you think we are? You'll need more than two men, if there's much carrying to be done. We stick."

"So do we," chimed in Fitz and I. "We'll get the message through, and get you through, too."

The major flushed and stood up.

"If that's the way you talk," he snapped (he was the black-eyed, quick kind, you know), "then I order that this march be resumed. Pack the burro. I order it."

"You'd better ride."

"I'll walk."

Well, he was our leader. We should obey, as long as he seemed capable. He was awfully stubborn, the major was, when he had his back up. But we exchanged glances, and we must all have thought the same: that if he was taken seriously again soon, and was laid out, we would try to persuade him to let us manage for him. Fitz only said quietly:

"But if you have to quit, you'll quit, won't you, Tom? You won't keep going, just to spite yourself. Real appendicitis can't be fooled with."

"I'll quit," he answered.

We packed Sally again, and started on. The major seemed to want to hike at the regulation fast Scouts' pace, but we held him in the best that we could. Anyway, after we had gone three or four miles, he was beginning to pant and double over; his pain had come back.

"I think I'll have to rest a minute," he said; and he sat down. "Go ahead. I'll catch up. You'd better take the message, Fitz. Here."

"No, sir," retorted Fitz. "If you think that we're going on and leave you alone, sick, you're off your base. This is a serious matter, Tom. It wouldn't be decent, and it wouldn't be Scout-like. The Red Foxes ought to go—"

"But we won't," they interrupted—

"—and we'll get you to some place where you can be attended to. Then we'll take the message, if you can't. There's plenty of time."

The major flushed and fidgeted, and fingered the package.

"Maybe I can ride, then," he offered. "We can cache more stuff and I'll ride Sally." He grunted and twisted as the pain cut him. He looked ghastly.

"He ought to lie quiet till we can take him some place and find a doctor," said Red Fox Scout Van Sant, emphatically. "There must be a ranch or a town around here."

"We'll ask this man coming," said Fitz.

The stream had met another, here, and so had the trail; and down the left-hand trail was riding at a little cow-pony trot a horseman. He was a cow-puncher. He wore leather chaps and spurs and calico shirt and flapping-brimmed drab slouch hat. When he reached us he reined in and halted. Hewas a middle-aged man, with freckles and sandy mustache.

"Howdy?" he said.

"Howdy?" we answered.

"Ain't seen any Big W cattle, back along the trail, have you?"

No, we hadn't — until suddenly I remembered.

"We saw some about ten days ago, on the other side of the Divide."

"Whereabouts?"

"On a mesa, northwest across the ridge from Dixon Park."

"Good eye," he grinned. "I heard some of our strays had got over into that country, but I wasn't sure."

We weren't here to talk cattle, though; and Fitz spoke up:

"Where's the nearest ranch, or town?"

"The nearest town is Shenandoah. That's on the railroad about eight miles yonder. Follow the right-hand trail and you'll come out on a wagon-road that takes you to it. But there's a ranch three miles up the valley by this other trail. Sick man?" The cow-puncher had good eyes, too.

"Yes. We want a doctor."

"Ain't any doctor at Shenandoah. That's nothing but a station and a store and a couple of houses. I expect the nearest doctor is the one at the mines."

"Where's that?"

"Fifteen miles into the hills, from the ranch."

"How far is Green Valley?" asked the major, weakly.

"Twenty-three or four miles, by this trail I come along. Same trail you take to the ranch. No doctor now at Green Valley, though. The one they had went back East."

"Then you let the Red Fox Scouts take me to the station and put me on the train for somewhere, and they can catch their own train; and you two fellows go ahead to Green Valley," proposed the major to Fitz.

"Ain't another train either way till to-morrow morning," said the cow-puncher. "They meet at Shenandoah, usually—when they ain't late. If you need a doctor, quickest way would be to make the ranch and ride to the mines and get him. What's the matter?"

"We don't know, for sure. Appendicitis, we think."

"Wouldn't monkey with it," advised the cow-puncher.

"Then the Red Foxes can hit for the railroad and Fitz and Jim and I'll make the ranch," insisted the major.

"We won't," spoke up Red Fox Scout Ward, flatly.

"We'll go with you to the ranch. We'll see this thing through. The railroad can wait."

"Well," said the cow-puncher, "you can't miss it. So long, and good luck."

"So long," we answered. He rode on, and we looked at the major.

"I suppose we ought to get you there as quick as we can," said Fitz, slowly. "Do you want to ride, or try walking again, or shall we carry you?"

"I'm better now," declared our plucky corporal. He stood up. "I'll walk, I guess. It isn't far."

So we set out, cautiously. No, it wasn't far—but it seemed mighty far. The major would walk a couple of hundred yards, and then he must rest. The pain doubled him right over. We took some of the stuff off Sally, and lifted him on top, but he couldn't stand that, either, very long. We tried a chair of our hands, but that didn't suit.

"I'll skip ahead and see if I can bring back a wagon, from the ranch," volunteered Red Fox Scout Van Sant; and away he ran. "You wait," he called back, over his shoulder.

We waited, and kept a cold pack on the major.

In about an hour and a half Van came panting back.

"There isn't any wagon," he gasped. "Nobody at the ranch except two women. Men folks have gone and taken the wagon with them."

That was hard. We skirmished about, and made a litter out of one of our blankets and two pieces of driftwood that we fished from the creek; andcarrying the major, with Sally following, we struck the best pace that we could down the trail. He was heavy, and we must stop often to rest ourselves and him; and we changed the cold packs.

At evening we toiled at last into the ranch yard. It had not been three miles: it had been a good long four miles.

CHAPTER XX

A FORTY-MILE RIDE

The ranch was only a small log shack, of two rooms, with corral and sheds and hay-land around it; it wasn't much of a place, but we were glad to get there. Smoke was rising from the stove-pipe chimney. As we drew up, one of the women looked out of the kitchen door, and the other stood in a shed with a milk-pail in her hand. The woman in the doorway was the mother; the other was the daughter. They were regular ranch women, hard workers and quick to be kind in an emergency. This was an emergency, for Major Henry was about worn out.

"Fetch him right in here," called the mother; and the daughter came hurrying.

We carried him into a sleeping room, and laid him upon the bed there. He had been all grit, up till now; but he quit and let down and lay there with eyes closed, panting.

"What is it?" they asked anxiously.

"He's sick. We think it's appendicitis."

"Oh, goodness!" they exclaimed. "What can we give him?"

"Nothing. Where can we get a doctor?"

"The mines is the nearest place, if he's there. That's twenty miles."

"But a man we met said it was fifteen."

"You can't follow that trail. It's been washed out. You'll have to take the other trail, around by the head of Cooper Creek."

"Can we get a saddle-horse here?"

"There are two in the corral; but I don't know as you can catch 'em. They're used to being roped."

"We'll rope them."

The major groaned. He couldn't help it.

"It's all right, old boy," soothed Fitz. "We'll have the doctor in a jiffy."

"Don't bother about me," gasped the major, without opening his eyes. "Go on through."

"You hush," we all retorted. "We'll do both: have you fixed up and get through, too."

The major fidgeted and complained weakly.

"One of us had better be catching the horses, hadn't we?" suggested Red Fox Scout Ward. "Van and I'll go for the doctor."

"No, you won't," said I. "I'll go. Fitz ought to stay. I know trails pretty well."

"Then either Van or I'll go with you. Two would be better than one."

"I'm going," declared Van Sant. "You stay here with Fitz, Hal."

That was settled. We didn't delay to dispute over the matter. There was work and duty for all.

"You be learning the trail, then," directed Fitz. "I'll be catching the horses."

"You'll find a rope on one of the saddles in the shed," called the daughter.

Fitz made for it; that was quicker than unpacking Sally and getting our own rope. Scout Ward went along to help. We tried to ease the major.

"You should have something to eat," exclaimed the women.

We said "no"; but they bustled about, hurrying up their own supper, which was under way when we arrived. While they bustled they fired questions at us; who we were, and where we had come from, and where we were going, and all.

The major seemed kind of light-headed. He groaned and wriggled and mumbled. The message was on his mind, and the Red Fox Scouts, and the fear that neither would get through in time. He kept trying to pass the message on to us; so finally I took it.

"All right. I've got it, major," I told him. "We'll carry it on. We can make Green Valley easy, from here. We'll start as soon as we can. To-morrow's Sunday, anyway. You go to sleep."

That half-satisfied him.

We found that we couldn't eat much. We drank some milk, and stuffed down some bread and butter; and by that time Fitz and Scout Ward had the horses led out. We heard the hoofs, and in came Ward, to tell us.

"Horses are ready," he announced.

Out we went. No time was to be lost. They even had saddled them—Fitz working with his one hand! So all we must do was to climb on. The women had told us the trail, and they had given us an old heavy coat apiece. Nights are cold, in the mountains.

"You know how, do you?" queried Fitz of me.

"Yes."

"That gray horse is the easiest," called one of the women, from the door.

"Let Jim take it, then," spoke Van.

But I had got ahead of him by grabbing the bay.

"Jim is used to riding," explained Fitz.

"So am I," answered Van.

"Not these saddles, Van," put in Ward. "They're different. The stirrups of the gray are longer, a little. They'll fit you better than they'll fit Jim."

Van had to keep the gray. It didn't matter to me which horse I rode, and it might to him from the East; so I was glad if the gray was the easier.

We were ready.

"We'll take care of Tom till you bring the doctor," said Fitz.

"We'll bring him."

"So long. Be Scouts."

"So long."

A quick grip of the hand from Fitz and Ward, and we were off, out of the light from the opened door where stood the two women, watching, and into the dimness of the light. Now for a forty-mile night ride, over a strange trail—twenty miles to the mines and twenty miles back. We would do our part and we knew that Fitz and Ward would do theirs in keeping the major safe.

That appeared a long ride. Twenty miles is a big stretch, at night, and when you are so anxious.

We were to follow on the main trail for half a mile until we came to a bridge. But before crossing the bridge there was a gate on the right, and a hay road through a field. After we had crossed the field we would pass out by another gate, and would take a trail that led up on top of the mesa. Then it was nineteen miles across the mesa, to the mines. The mines would have a light. They were running night and day.

We did not say much, at first. We went at fast walk and little trots, so as not to wind the horses in the very beginning. We didn't dash away, headlong, as you sometimes read about, or see in pictures. I knew better. Scouts must understand how to treat a horse, as well as how to treat themselves, on the march.

This was a dark night, because it was cloudy. There were no stars, and the moon had not come up yet. So we must trust to the horses to keep the trail. By looking close we could barely see it, in spots. Of course, the darkness was not a deep black darkness. Except in a storm, the night of the open always is thinnish, so you can see after your eyes are used to it.

I had the lead. Up on the mesa we struck into a trot. A lope is easier to ride, but the trot is the natural gait of a horse, and he can keep up a trot longer than he can a lope. Horses prefer trotting to galloping.

Trot, trot, trot, we went.

"How you coming?" I asked, to encourage Van.

"All right," he grunted. "These stirrups are too long, though. I can't get any purchase."

"Doesn't your instep touch, when you stand up in them?"

"If I straighten out my legs. I'm riding on my toes. That's the way I was taught. I like to have my knees crooked so I can grip with them. Don't you, yours?"

"Just to change off to, as a rest. But cowboys and other people who ride all day stick their feet through the stirrup to the heel, and ride on their instep. A crooked leg gives a fellow a cramp in the knee, after a while. Out here we ride straight up and down, so we are almost standing in the stirrups all the time. That's the cowboy way, and it's about the cavalry way, too. Those men know."

"How do you grip, then?"

"With the thigh. Try it. But when you're trotting you'd better stand in the stirrups and you can lean forward on the horn, for a rest."

Van grunted. He was experimenting.

"Should think it would make your back ache," he said.

"What?"

"To ride with such long stirrups."

"Uh uh," I answered. "Not when you sit up and balance in the saddle and hold your spine straight. It always makes my back ache to hunch over. We Elk Scouts try to ride with heel and shoulders in line. We can ride all day."

"Humph!" grunted Van. "Let's lope."

"All right."

So we did lope, a little way. Then we walked another little way, and then I pushed into the same old trot. That was hard on Van, but it was what would cover the ground and get us through quickest to the doctor. So we must keep at it.

Sometimes I stood in the stirrups and leaned on the horn; sometimes I sat square and "took it."

We crossed the mesa, and first thing we knew, we were tilting down into a gulch. The horses picked their way slowly; we let them. We didn't want any tumbles or sprained legs. The bottom of the gulch held willows and aspens and brush, and was dark, because shut in. We didn't trot. My old horse just put his nose down close to the ground, and went along at an amble, like a dog, smelling the trail. I let the lines hang and gave him his head. Behind me followed Van and his gray. I could hear the gray also sniffing.

"Will we get through?" called Van, anxiously. "Think we're still on the trail?"

"Sure," I answered.

Just then my horse snorted, and raised his head and snorted more, and stood stock-still, trembling. I could feel that his ears were pricked. He acted as if he was seeing something, in the trail.

"Gwan!" I said, digging him with my heels.

"What's the matter?" called Van.

His horse had stopped and was snorting.

"Don't know."

It was pitchy dark. I strained to see, but I couldn't. That is a creepy thing, to have your horse act so, when you don't know why. Of course you think bear and cougar. But we were not to be held up by any foolishness, and I was not a bit afraid.

"Gwan!" I ordered again.

"Gwan!" repeated Van.

I heard a crackling in the brush, and my horse proceeded, sidling and snorting past the spot. Van's gray followed, acting the same way. It might have been a bear; we never knew.

On we went, winding through the black timber again. We were on the trail, all right; for by looking at the tree-tops against the sky we could just see them and could see that they were always opening out, ahead. The trail on the ground was kind of reproduced on the sky.

It was a long way, through that dark gulch. But nothing hurt us and we kept going.

The gulch widened; we rode through a park, and the horses turned sharply and began to climb a hill—zigzagging back and forth. We couldn't see a trail, and I got off and felt with my hands.

A trail was there.

We came out on top. Here it was lighter. The moon had risen, and some light leaked through the clouds.

"Do you think we're on the right trail, still?" asked Van, dubiously. "They didn't say anything about this other hill."

That was so. But they hadn't said anything about there being two trails, either. They had said that when we struck the trail over the mesa, to follow it to the mines.

"It must be the right trail," I said, back. "All we can do is to keep following it."

Seemed to me that we had gone the twenty miles already. But of course we hadn't.

"Maybe we've branched off, on to another trail," persisted Van. "The horses turned, you remember. Maybe we ought to go back and find out."

"No, it's the right trail," I insisted, again. "There's only the one, they said."

We must stick to that thought. We had been told by persons who knew. If once we began to fuss and not believe, and experiment, then we both would get muddled and we might lose ourselves completely. I remembered what old Jerry the prospector once had said: "When you're on a trail, and you've been told that it goes somewhere, keep it till you get there. Nobody can describe a trail by inches."

We went on and on and on. It was down-hill and up-hill and across and through; but we pegged along. Van was about discouraged; and it was a horrible sensation, to suspect that after all we might have got upon a wrong trail, and that we were not heading for the doctor but away from him, while Fitz and Ward were doing their best to save Tom, thinking that we would come back bringing the doctor.

We didn't talk much. Van was dubious, and I was afraid to discuss with him, or I might be discouraged, too. I put all my attention to making time at fast walk and at trot, and in hoping. Jiminy, how I did hope. Every minute or two I was thinking that I saw a light ahead—the light of the mines. But when it did appear, it appeared all of a sudden, around a shoulder: a light, and several lights, clustered, in a hollow before!

"There it is, Van!" I cried; and I was so glad that I choked up.

"Is that the mines?"

"Sure. Must be. Hurrah!"

"Hurrah!"

The sight changed everything. Now the night wasn't dark, the way hadn't been so long after all, we weren't so tired, we had been silly to doubt the trail; for we had arrived, and soon we would be talking with the doctor.

The trail wound and wound, and suddenly, again, it entered in among sheds, and the dumps of mines. At the first light I stopped. The door was partly open. It was the hoisting house of a mine, and the engineer was looking out, to see who we were.

"Is the doctor here?" I asked.

"Guess so. Want him?"

"Yes."

"He has a room over the store. Somebody hurt? Where you from?"

"Harden's ranch. Where is the store?"

"I'll show you. Here." He led the way. "Somebody hurt over there?"

"No. Sick."

We halted beside a platform of a dim building, and the engineer pounded on the door.

"Oh, doc!" he called.

And when that doctor answered, through the window above, and we knew that it was he, and that we had him at last, I wanted to laugh and shout. But now we must get him back to the major.

"You're needed," explained the man. "Couple of kids." And he said to us: "Go ahead and tell him. I'm due at the mine." And off he trudged. We thanked him.

"What's the trouble?" asked the doctor.

"Appendicitis, we think. We're from the Harden ranch."

"Great Scott!" we heard the doctor mutter. Then he said. "All right, I'll be down." And we waited.

He came out of a side door and around upon the porch. He was buttoning his shirt.

"Who's got it? Not one of you?"

"No, another boy. He was sick on the trail and we took him to the ranch. Then we rode over here."

"What makes you think your friend has appendicitis?"

We described how the major acted and what Fitz had found out by feeling, and what we had done.

"Sounds suspicious," said the doctor, shortly. "You did the right thing, anyway. Do you want to go back with me? I'll start right over. Expect you're pretty tired."

"We'll go," we both exclaimed. We should say so! We wanted to be there, on the spot.

"I'll just get my case, and saddle-up." And he disappeared.

He was a young doctor, smooth-faced; I guess he hadn't been out of college very long; but he was prompt and ready. He came down in a moment with a lantern, and put his case on the porch. He handed us a paper of stuff.

"There's some lump sugar," he said. "Eat it. I always carry some about with me, on long rides. It's fine for keeping up the strength."

He swung the lantern to get a look at us, then he went back toward the stables, and saddled his horse. He was in the store a moment, too.

"I've got some cheese," he announced, when he came out again. "Cheese and sugar don't sound good as a mixture, but they'll see us through. We must keep our nerve, you know. All aboard?"

"All aboard," we answered.

That was another long ride, back; but it did not seem so long as the ride in, because we knew that we were on the right trail. The doctor talked and asked us all about our trip as Scouts, and told experiences that he had had on trips, himself; and we tried to meet him at least halfway. But all the time I was wondering about the major, and whether we would reach him in time, and whether he would get well, and what was happening now, there. But there was no use in saying this, or in asking the doctor a lot of questions. He would know and he would do his best, and so would we all.

Just at daylight we again entered the ranch yard. Fitz waved his one arm from the ranch door. He came to meet us. His eyes were sticky and swollen and his face pale and set, but he smiled just the same.

"Here's the doctor," we reported. "How is he?"

"Not so bad, as long as we keep the cold compress on. He's slept."

"Good," said the doctor. "We'll fix him up now, all right."

He swung off, with his case, and Fitz took him right in. Van and I sort of tumbled off, and stumbled along after. Those forty miles at trot and fast walk had put a crimp in our legs. But I tell you, we were thankful that we had done it!

And here was our second Sunday.

CHAPTER XXI

THE LAST DASH

That young doctor was fine. He took things right into his own hands, and Major Henry said all right. The major was weak but game. He was gamer than any of us. Fitz and Red Fox Scout Ward had slept some by turns, and the two women were ready to help, too; but the doctor gave Red Fox Scout Van Sant and me the choice of going to sleep or going fishing.

It was Sunday and we didn't need the fish. We didn't intend to go to sleep; we just let them show us a place, in the bunk-house, and we lay down, for a minute. For we were ready to help, as well as the rest of them. A Scout must not be afraid of blood or wounds. We only lay down with a blanket over us, instead of going fishing — and when I opened my eyes again the sun was bright and Fitz and Ward were peeking in on us.

They were pale, but they looked happy.

Van and I tried to sit up.

"Is it over with?" we asked.

"Sure."

"Did he take it out? Was that what was the matter?"

"Yes. Want to see it?"

No, we didn't. I didn't, anyway.

"How is he? Can we see him?"

"The doctor says he'll be all right. Maybe you can see him. He's out from under. It's one o'clock."

One o'clock! Phew! We were regular deserters — but we hadn't intended to be.

We tumbled out, now, and hurried to wash and fix up, so that we would look good to the major. Sick people are finicky. The daughter was in the kitchen, but the mother and the doctor were eating. There was a funny sweetish smell, still; smell of chloroform. It is a serious smell, too.

The doctor smiled at us. "I ought to have taken yours out, while you were asleep," he joked. "I've been thinking of it."

"Is he all right?" we asked; Fitz and Ward behind us, ready to hear again.

"Bully, so far."

"Indeed he is," added the mother.

"Can we see him?"

"You can stand on the threshold and say one word: 'Hello.'"

We tiptoed through. The bed was clean and white, with a sheet outside instead of the colored spread; and the major was in it. The Elks' flag was spread out, draped over the dresser, where he could see it. His eyes opened at us. He didn't look so very terrible, and he tried to grin.

"How?" he said.

"Hello," said we; and we gave him the Scouts' sign.

"Didn't even make me sick," he croaked. "But I can't get up. Don't you fellows wait. You go ahead."

"We will," we said, to soothe him. Then we gave him the Scouts' sign again, and the silence sign, and the wolf sign (for bravery) , and we drew back. The doctor had told us that we could say one word, and we had been made to say three!

We had seen that the major was alive and up and coming (not really up; only going to be, you know); but this was another anxious day, I tell you! Having an appendix cut out is no light matter, ever—and besides, here was the fourteenth day on the trail! The major would not be able to stir for a week and a half, maybe; yet Green Valley, our goal, was only twenty-one miles away!

"It's all a question of the nursing that he has now, boys," said the doctor, in council with us. "I'm going to trust that to you Scouts; these women have all they can do, anyway. We got the appendix out just in time — but if it hadn't been for your first-aid treatment in the beginning we might havebeen too late. That old appendix was swollen and ready to burst if given half a chance. His pure Scout's blood and his Scout's vitality will pull him through O. K. That's what he gets, from living right, following out Scouts' rules. But he must have attention night and day according to hygiene. We don't want any microbes monkeying with that wound I made."

"No, you bet," we said.

"I'll leave you complete directions and then I'm going back to the mines; but I'll ride over again to-morrow morning. Can't you keep him from fussing about that message?"

"We'll try," we said.

"If you can't, then one of you can jump on a horse and take it over, so as to satisfy him. You can make the round trip in five hours."

Well, we were pledged not to do that; horse or other help was forbidden. But we did not say so. What was the use? And it didn't seem now as though either Fitz or I could stand it to leave the major even for five hours. The Red Fox Scouts of course must skip on, to the railroad, or they'd miss their big Yellowstone trip, and we two Elks would be on night and day duty, with the major. The doctor said that he would be out of danger in five days. By that time the message would be long overdue. It was too bad. We had tried so hard.

The doctor left us written directions, until he should come back; and he rode off for the mines.

Fitz and I took over the nursing, and let the two women go on about their ranch work. They were mighty nice to us, and we didn't mean to bother them any more than was absolutely necessary. The two Red Foxes stayed a while longer. They said that they would light out early in the morning, if the major had a good night, in time to catch the train all right. But they didn't; we might have smelled a mouse, if we hadn't been so anxious about the major. They were good as gold, those two Red Foxes.

You see, the major kept fussing. He was worried over the failure of the message. He had it on his mind all the time. To-morrow was the fifteenth day—and here we were, laid up because of him. We told him no matter; we all had done our Scouts' best, and no fellows could have done more. But we would stick by him. That was our Scouts' duty, now.

He kept fussing. When we took his temperature, as the doctor had ordered, it had gone up two degrees. That was bad. We could not find any other special symptoms. His cut didn't hurt him, and he had not a thing to complain of—except that we wouldn't carry the message through in time.

"You'll have to do it," said Red Fox Scout Van Sant to Fitz and me.

"But we can't."

"Why not?"

That was a silly question for a Scout to ask.

"We can't leave Tom."

"Yes, you can. Hal and I are here."

"You've got to make that train, right away."

"No, we haven't."

"But you'll miss the Yellowstone trip!"

"We can take it later."

"No, sir! That won't do. The major and we, and the general, too, if he knew, won't have it that way at all. You fellows have been true Scouts. Now you go ahead."

Scout Van flushed and fidgeted.

"Well, to tell the truth," he blurted, "I guess we've missed connections a little anyway. But we don't care. We sent a telegram in this afternoon by the doctor to our crowd, telling them to go ahead themselves and not to expect us until we cut their trail. The doctor will telephone it to the operator."

We gasped.

"You see," continued Van, "we two Red Foxes can take care of the major while you're gone, like a brick. We're first-aid nurses, and the doctor has told us what to do; and he's coming back to-morrow and the next day you'll be back, maybe. He said that if the major fussed you'd better do what's wanted."

"But look here—!" began Fitz. "The major'll feel worse if he knows you're missing your trip than if the message is delayed a day or two."

"No, he won't," argued Van. "We'll explain to him. We won't miss our trip. We'll catch the crowd somewhere. Besides, that's only pleasure. This other is business. You're on the trail, in real Scouts' service, to show what Scouts can do, so we want to help."

It seemed to me that they were showing what Scouts can do, too! They were splendid, those Red Foxes.

"The major'll just fuss and fret, you know," finished Van. "That's what has sent his temperature up, already."

"Well," said Fitz, slowly, "we'll see. We Elks appreciate how you other Scouts have stuck and helped. Don't we, Jim?"

"We sure do," I agreed. "But we don't want to ride a free horse to death."

"Bosh!" laughed Van. "We're all Scouts. That's enough."

Red Fox Scout Ward beckoned to us.

"The major wants you," he said.

We went in. The major did not look good to me. His cheeks were getting flushed and his eyes were large and rabbity.

"I can't quiet him," claimed Ward, low, as we entered.

"Do you know this is the fourteenth day?" piped the major. "I've been counting up and it is. I'm sure it is."

"That's all right, old boy," soothed Fitz. "You let us do the counting. All you need do is get well."

"But we have to put that message through, don't we?" answered the major. "Just because I'm laid up is no reason why the rest of you must be laid up, too. Darn it! Can't you do something?"

He was excited. That was bad.

"I've been thinking," proceeded the major. "The general was hurt, and dropped out, but we others went on. Then little Jed Smith was hurt, and he and Kit Carson dropped out, but we others went on. And now I'm hurt, and I've dropped out, and none of you others will go on. That seems mighty mean. I don't see why you're trying to make me responsible. Everybody'll blame me."

"Of course they won't," I said.

He was wriggling his feet and moving his arms, and he was almost crying.

"Would you get well quick if we leave you and take the message through, Tom?" asked Fitz, suddenly.

The major quit wriggling, and his face shone.

"Would I? I'd beat the record. I'd sleep all I'm told to, and eat soup, and never peep. Will you, Fitz? Sure?"

"To-morrow morning. You lie quiet, and quit fussing, and sleep, and be a model patient in the hospital, and then to-morrow morning early we'll hike."

"Both of you?"

"Yep."

"One isn't enough, in case you meet trouble. It's two on the trail, for us Scouts."

"I know it."

"And you'll take the flag? I want the Elks flag to go."

"We will," we said.

"To-morrow morning, then," and the major smiled a peaceful, happy little smile. "Bueno. Now I'll go to sleep. You needn't give me any dope. I'll see you off in the morning." And he sort of settled and closed his eyes. "When are you Red Foxes off?" he asked drowsily.

"Oh, we've arranged to be around here a day yet," drawled Van Sant. "You can't get rid of us. We want to hear that the message went through. Then we'll skip. We ought to rest one day in seven. And there's a two-pound trout in a hole here, Mrs. Harden says, and Hal thinks he can catch him to-morrow before I do."

"You mustn't miss that trip," murmured the major. And when we tiptoed out, leaving Fitz on guard, he was asleep already!

So it seemed that we had done the best thing.

Red Foxes Ward and Van Sant divided the night watch between them so that we Elks should be fresh for the day's march. We were up early, and got our own breakfast, so as not to bother the two women; but the report came out from the major's room that he had had a bully night, and that now he was awake and was bound to see us. So we went in.

He had the Elks flag in his hands.

"Who's got that message?" he asked.

I had, you know.

He passed the flag to Fitz.

"You take this, then. You're sure going, aren't you?"

"Yes, sir."

"All right. You can make it. Don't you worry about me. I'm fine. Be Scouts. It's the last leg."

"You be a Scout, too. If we're to be Scouts, on the march, you ought to be a Scout, in the hospital."

"I will." He knew what we meant. "But I wish I could go."

"So do we."

"All ready?"

"All ready."

He shook our hands.

"So long."

"So long."

We gave him the Scouts' salute, and out we went. We shook hands with the Red Foxes; they saluted us, and we saluted them. We crossed the yard for the trail; and when we looked back, the two women waved at us. We waved back. And now we were carrying the message again, with only twenty-one miles to go.

The trail was up grade, following beside the creek, and we knew that we must allow at least eight hours for those twenty-one miles. It was not to be a nice day, either. Mists were floating around among the hills, which was a pretty certain sign of rain.

We hiked on. I had the message, hanging inside my shirt. It felt good. I suspected that Fitz ought to be the one to carry it; he was my superior. But he didn't ask for it, and I tried to believe that my carrying it made no difference to him. I was thinking about offering it to him, but I didn't. He had his camera, and the flag wrapped about his waist like a sash. We'd left Sally and our other stuff at the ranch, and were traveling light for this last spurt.

It was a wagon trail right down the valley, and we could travel fast. The sun grew hotter, and a hole in my boot-sole began to raise a blister on my foot. Those fourteen days of steady trailing had been hard on leather, and on clothes, too.

We passed several ranches. Along in the middle of the morning thunder began to growl in the hills, and we knew that we were liable to be wet.

The valley grew narrower, as if it was to pinch out, and the thunder grew louder. The storm was rising black over the hills ahead of us.

"That's going to be a big one," said Fitz.

It looked so. The clouds were the rolling, tumbling kind, where drab and black are mixed. And they came fast, to eat the sun.

It was raining hard on the hills ahead. We could see the lightning every second, awful zigzags and splits and bursting bombs, and the thunder was one long bellow.

The valley pinched to not much more than a gulch, with aspens and pines and willows, and now and then little grassy places, and the stream rippling down through the middle. Half the sky was gone, now, and the sun was swallowed, and it was time that Fitz and I found cover. We did not hunt a tree; not much! Trees are lightning attracters, and they leak, besides. But we saw where a ledge of shelf-rock cropped out, making a little cave.

"We'd better get in here and cache till the worst is over," proposed Fitz. "We'll eat our lunch while we're waiting."

That sounded like sense. So we snuggled under. We could just sit up, with our feet inside the edge.

"Boom-oom-oom!" roared the thunder, shaking the ground.

"Boom-oom-oom! Oom! Oom! Boom!"

We could feel a chill, the breeze stopped, as if scared, drops began to patter, a few, and then more, faster and faster, hard and swift as hail, the world got dark, and suddenly with roar and slash down she came, while we were eating our first sandwich put up by the two women.

That was the worst rain that Fitz or I had ever seen. Between mouthfuls we watched. The drops were big and they fell like a spurt from a hose, until all the outside world was just one sheet of water. The streaks drummed with the rumble of a hundred wagons. We couldn't see ten feet. Before we had eaten our second sandwiches, the water was trickling through cracks in the shelf-rock roof, and dirt was washing away from the sides of our cave. Outside, the land was a stretch of yellow, liquid adobe, worked upon by the fierce pour.

"We'll have to get out of this," shouted Fitz in my ear. "This roof may cave in on us."

And out he plunged; I followed. We were soaked through in an instant, and I could feel the water running down my skin. We could scarcely see where to go or what to do; but we had bolted just in time. One end of the shelf-rock washed out like soap, and in crumpled the roof, as a mass of shale and mud! Up the gulch sounded a roaring—another, different roaring from the roaring of the rain and thunder. Fitz grabbed my hand.

"Run!" he shouted. "Quick! Get across!"

This was no time for questions, of course. I knew that he spoke in earnest, and had some good reason. Hand in hand we raced, sliding and slipping, for the creek. It had changed a heap in five minutes. It was all a thick yellow, and was swirling and yeasty. Fitz waded right in, in a big hurry to get on the other side. He let go of my hand, but I followed close. The current bit at my knees, and we stumbled on the hidden rocks. Out Fitz staggered, and up the opposite slope, through sage and bushes. The roaring was right behind us. It was terrible. We were about all in, and Fitz stopped, panting.

"See that?" he gasped, pointing back.

A wave of yellow muck ten feet high was charging down the gulch like a squadron of cavalry in solid formation. Logs and tree-branches were sticking out of it, and great rocks were tossing and floating. Another second, and it had passed, and where we had come from—trail and shelf-rock and creek—was nothing but the muddy water and driftwood tearing past, with the pines and aspens and willows trembling amidst it. But it couldn't reach us.

"Cloud-burst," called Fitz, in my ear.

I nodded. He was white. I felt white, too. That had been a narrow escape.

"We could have climbed that other side, couldn't we?" I asked.

"We were on the wrong side of the creek, though. We might have been cut off from where we're going. That's what I thought of. See?"

Wise old Fitz. That was Scouty, to do the best thing no matter how quick you must act. Of course, with the creek between us and Green Valley, and the bridges washed out and the water up, we might have been held back for half a day!

The yellow flood boiled below, but the rain was quitting, and we might as well move on, anyway.

According to what we had been told of the trail, up at the head of the gulch it turned off, and crossed the creek on a high bridge, and made through the hills northwest for the town. Now we must shortcut to strike it over in that direction.

The rain was quitting; the sun was going to shine. That was a hard climb, through the wet and the stickiness and the slipperiness, with our clothes weighting us and clinging to us and making us hotter. But up we pushed, puffing. Then we followed the ridge a little way, until we had to go down. Next we must go up again, for another ridge.

Fitz plugged along; so did I. The sun came out and the ground steamed, and our clothes gradually dried, as the brush and trees dried; but somehow

I didn't feel extra good. My head thumped, and things looked queer. It didn't result in anything serious, after the hike was over, so I guess that maybe I was hungry and excited. The rain had soaked our lunch as well as us and we threw it away in gobs; we counted on supper in Green Valley.

We didn't stop. Fitz was going strong. He was steel. And if I could hold out I mustn't say a word. So it was up-hill and down-hill, across country through brush and scattered timber, expecting any time to hit the trail or come in sight of the town. And how my head did thump!

Finally in a draw we struck a cow-path, and we stuck to this, because it looked as if it was going somewhere. Other cow-paths joined it, and it got larger and larger and more hopeful; and about five o'clock by the sun we stepped into a main traveled road. Hurrah! This was the trail for us.

The rain had not spread this far, and the road was dusty. A signboard said, pointing: "Brown's Big Store, Green Valley's Leader, One Mile." We were drawing near! I tried not to limp, and not to notice my head, as we spurted to a fast walk, straight-foot and quick, so that we would enter triumphantly. As like as not people would be looking out for us, as this was the last day; and we would show them Scouts' spirit. We Elks had fought treachery and fire and flood, and we had left four good men along the way; those had been a strenuous fifteen days, but we were winning through at last.

That last mile seemed to me longer than any twenty. The dust and gravel were hot, the sun flamed, my blister felt like a cushion full of needles, my legs were heavy and numb, that old head thumped like a drum, and I had a notion that if I slackened or lost my stride I'd never finish out that mile. So when Fitz stumbled on a piece of rock, and his strap snapped and he stopped to pick up his camera, I kept moving. He would catch me.

A shoulder of rock stuck out and the road curved around it; and when I had curved around it, too, then I saw something that sent my heart into my throat, and brought me up short. With two leaps I was back, around the rock again, in time to sign Fitz, coming: "Halt! Silence!" And I motioned him close behind the shoulder.

Beyond the rock the road stretched straight and clear, with the town only a quarter of a mile. But only about a hundred yards away, where the creek flowed close to the road, were two fellows, fishing. One was Bill Duane!

Fitz obeyed my signs. He gazed at me, startled and anxious.

"What is it?" he asked, pantomime.

I held up two fingers, for two enemies. Then I cautiously peeked out. Bill Duane was leaving the water, as if he was coming; and the other fellow was coming. The other fellow was Mike Delavan. They must have seen me before I had jumped back. We might have circuited them, but now it was too late. I never could stand a chase over the hills, and maybe Fitz couldn't.

But there was a way, and a chance, and I made up my mind in a twinkling. I jerked out the message and held it at Fitz. He shook his head. I signed what we would do—what I would do and what he must do. He shook his head. He wouldn't. We would stick together. I clinched my teeth and waved my fist under his nose, and signed that he must. He was the one.

Then I thrust the message into his hand, and out I sprang. Around the shoulder of rock Bill and Mike were sneaking, to see what had become of me. They were only about fifty yards, now, and I made for them as if to dodge them. They let out a yell and closed in, and up the hill at one side I pegged. They pegged to head me.

My legs worked badly. I didn't mind breaking the blister (I felt the warm stuff ooze out, and the sting that followed); but those heavy legs! As a Scout I ought to have skipped up the hill as springy and long-winded as a goat; but instead I had to shove myself. But up I went, nip and tuck—and my head thumped when my heart did, about a thousand times a minute. Every step I took hurt from hair to sole. But I didn't care, if I only could go far enough. Bill and Mike climbed after, on the oblique so as to cut me off before I could reach the top of the ridge and the level there.

Straight up I went, drawing them on; and halfway my throat was too dry and my legs were too heavy and my head jarred my eyes too much, and I wobbled and fell down. On came the two enemy; but I didn't care. I looked past them and saw Fitzpatrick the Bad Hand pelting down the road. He had cached his camera, but he had the flag and the message, his one arm was working like a driving-rod, he was running true, the trail lay straight and waiting, with the goal open, and I knew that he would make it!